the DEEP BLUE Between

Ayesha Harruna Attah

Pushkin Press
71–75 Shelton Street
London WC2H 9JQ

The Deep Blue Between was first published by Pushkin Press in 2020

1 3 5 7 9 8 6 4 2

ISBN 13: 978-1-78269-266-9

Designed and typeset by Tetragon, London
Printed and bound by CPI Group (UK) Ltd, Croydon, CR0 4YY

www.pushkinpress.com

For Tumi and Tami

CHAPTER ONE

In our dreams, our father sits in a room where colour doesn't live. Our mother suckles her baby, but both their limbs are frozen as if forgotten by time. Fire burns up our village, smoke chokes our throats, flames sear our skin. We run. Our hands clasp each other's with the hold of glue. Her fingers are my fingers; my fingers are hers. Ours is a grip that started in the womb, before our first separation. We have lost home before, but that didn't break us. Now, we are losing home again, but we still have each other. We run. Chased by hooves and cries and winged men. One of us trips. Sweat lubricates the thin film between our hands. Her fingers slide down mine. We were wrong. This time, it feels final. She slips away from me.

CHAPTER TWO

Hassana

I could start with how my baba went to sell his shoes in Jenne and never came back. Or how our village was crisped to the ground and how I don't know of my mother or grandmother's whereabouts. Or how my big sister Aminah and I lost our brother in a human caravan. Or I could tell you about the worst day of my life, when my twin sister was snatched from me. But I'll start with the moment I stopped letting other people control what I did or where I went or what happened to me. I will start with the moment I broke free.

In 1892, when I was ten, I was forced to live on a land where the trees grew so close together, they sucked out my voice. Wofa Sarpong, a man as tall as me, had bought Aminah and me, and brought us to his home in a clearing surrounded by trees that scraped the sky. Every time I looked up, I wondered how the trees stayed up so tall and didn't topple over, and every day, the forest squeezed my chest flat like an empty cow-skin gourd. Many nights, I would wake up sweating, heart racing, and always breathless. I was a child of the savannah, of open spaces and short trees. From the horizon, we could see the camels of the caravan arriving. The world seemed vast and limitless. The forest shrank the world and my whole life with it.

There isn't one thing I can say I liked about Wofa Sarpong and his family. Maybe only that Aminah was still there with me. She fared slightly better than me, and said Wofa Sarpong's food was quite tasty, that their tuo, which they called fufu, was sweeter than ours. She made sure I sipped their soups with fish and mushrooms, but I could have been eating the bark of a tree. It all felt heavy against my tongue; it all had no flavour. I ate because Aminah told me to. But I was half a person.

The change in my story began at the height of kola season. Wofa Sarpong had made us climb up more kola trees than I could count, as always. We little ones—his children and the ones he'd bought—scrambled up like lizards, in search of spots far away from each other to better harvest as many of the pods as we could. Wofa Sarpong said kola was God's gift, and God would be angry if we didn't take all that he'd given us. *I* was angry at Otienu, my God, for sending me to a place like this when I had done nothing wrong. Sometimes, I wondered what Wofa Sarpong's God was like. He seemed to be blessing Wofa Sarpong with an abundance of kola nuts. I will never forget having to stretch out my arms to cut the pods of kola at their bases, while precariously balancing my bare feet on branches, each time thinking I would fall. I never did fall and managed to still my fear enough to keep grabbing the pods, which I threw down to Kwesi, Aminah and the other older ones, who put them into big baskets they would later carry. Every day, we

9

worked morning and afternoon, and Wofa Sarpong never thanked us for our work.

When he said, "All done", it was our cue to climb back down. We dropped our knives in big baskets, on top of kola pods with their gnarled-looking shells. We walked back on a path criss-crossed with ants every couple of steps we took. I could watch ants for days. The way they went about their work one at a time, and how if one of them got into trouble, they all came together to help. That day, I was filled with incredible sadness, remarking to myself how such tiny creatures could show kindness to each other, while people like Wofa Sarpong and the men who had kidnapped us were filled with nothing but cruelty.

We got to Wofa Sarpong's compound of four wide huts—for him and his wives and young children—and two on the other side, for his grown children and those of us he'd bought. Close to the opening of his home was a hut that stood alone, where food pots and mortars and pestles were kept. As Aminah walked ahead with her basket, I went into that solitary hut and took a black earthenware pot to Wofa Sarpong's first wife. I felt heavy, as if a blacksmith's anvil had been tied to my back. Wofa Sarpong's wife scooped two glistening mounds of tuo and put them in the pot and passed the bowl to her co-wife, who fetched ladlefuls of palm soup with two specks of fish.

"Smile!" she commanded.

Usually, I would paste a half-smile on my face, something to shake them off, but that day I couldn't even try.

I put the pot before Aminah and the other girls and they

dipped their fingers in the soup and began eating. Before I could decide whether I wanted to eat or not, Aminah had led the tuo to my lips.

"Eat your fufu," she said.

I refused to use their words. I would not call it fufu like Aminah.

I took the lump of yellow plantain and cassava to my mouth and it tasted like air, then seconds later, my stomach churned. The food would come up if I kept trying, so I got up and went to sit under the abrofo nkatie tree. I wanted it all to end.

We had been brought over about a year before, and the sounds of the night still made me jump. Wofa Sarpong stole into our room often to see Aminah and after he left, I stayed awake listening to my sister cry by my side. That night, even though I hadn't eaten a thing, under the weight of my sadness, I slept like a fully fed python.

All around us is water reflecting a blue that is deeper than the sky. There are people around us looking at the water, which behind us stretches past the edges of the earth. There are cloths blowing like big white scarves in the wind and we are standing on a wooden platform. Ahead of us is land that looks familiar and unfamiliar all at once, with palm-like trees that shake and bend in the wind. The trees grow bigger and bigger. We are moving.

I woke up, my clothes wet, as if a bucket of water had been flung on me. The forest had not only taken my voice—it had seeped into my dreams, severing the strongest connection I shared with my sister. When our baba disappeared, we knew he was alive because Husseina and I both dreamt he was in a room. I would see things from one angle. She would see things from the other. If I saw a face, she saw a back. Together, we saw whole. The forest had made our dreams lose their way to each other. Until now…

I shook Aminah awake and told her about the dream.

"These are her dreams," I said. "Husseina is alive."

The days that followed were different. The weight of sadness lifted, replaced with a confusing mix of excitement and a terrible pain in my belly. My stomach's aches doubled as I washed the Sarpong family's clothes, and as I climbed up kola trees. I couldn't sit still or focus, especially as Wofa Sarpong lined us up and told us something and even when Aminah spoke to me. My twin was alive and in a place surrounded by the bluest water I'd ever seen. One minute, I felt I should run and hug everyone, announcing the news; the next, fear washed over me—what if we never saw each other again, with only our dreams threading us to each other? Could I live with that? The question haunted me, twisting my insides into painful knots.

One afternoon, while we were winnowing millet, Wofa Sarpong, accompanied by a man I had never seen on the farm, gathered everyone in the courtyard where his children hid sticks and stones and where I was already sitting. The newcomer wore short shorts held up high on his waist by a leather rope. He also wore a white hat and paced up and down as he waited for Wofa Sarpong to organize us. The man went round asking everyone's names, and I barely listened. I wanted to get back to looking for weevils and stones. I couldn't stop thinking about Husseina.

Someone poked me in the sides.

The man in the shorts and cap asked me my name.

"Hassana," I said.

Wofa Sarpong looked at me as if I had stolen the last piece of fish in his soup.

The man asked me again.

"Hassana." This time I meant it, realizing that when Wofa Sarpong had assembled us earlier, it was to give us new names. He didn't want to be caught for keeping slaves. Our names gave us up. I told the man I was from Botu, that I was the second daughter of Baba Yero and Aminah-Na.

Wofa Sarpong followed the man, bowing so low it looked like he would scrape the ground and, for the first time since arriving on his farm, I wanted to laugh. I went back to my weevils and stones.

I taught myself to hold my breath underwater when I was seven. No women in Botu could swim, but it was as if I knew that I would have to hold my breath many times. One time, it made me the bravest girl in all of Botu. The girls and I were at the waterhole early in the morning to fetch water. Suddenly, I heard shrieking. One word emerged out of the rush of voices: crocodile. We didn't have crocodiles at the waterhole. After the girls had rushed out of the water, I held my breath and ducked into the water. At first, silt rose

13

up and clouded the water. I kept my breath contained in my chest as I waited for the mud to settle. The water grew clearer and I saw human legs under the crocodile hide. I lifted my head out of the water. The girls were shouting.

"Hassana, come out!" Somebody's loud voice floated above the rest.

I watched the crocodile hide approach me, and I looked back, caught eyes with Husseina, who had squeezed her face, ready to burst into tears. Then I returned to the crocodile, which was now right in front of me. We'd see how long this game could go on. The girls' cries had become a ringing in my ears: "GET-OUT-GET-OUT-GET-OUT". The sun fried my back. The snout of the grey creature started to move higher. The girls screeched. The crocodile skin floated up, turned sideways, and splashed into the water, revealing Motaaba with his big teeth. He doubled over and laughed as I walked out of the water and took Husseina's hand. She laid her head on my shoulder and didn't say anything as we walked back home.

When Wofa Sarpong came back from seeing off the inspector, he was holding the whip he used on his donkey. He dragged me away from my bowl of millet. When he started whipping me I screamed at first, but when I heard the ugly sound of defeat coming out of my mouth, I held my breath. His whacks did nothing to me. If anything, they gave me the push I was looking for. I would no longer stay in this place to be treated like one of his donkeys. I was leaving to find Husseina. Aminah could come if she wanted, but if she wanted to be treated like an animal, she could stay.

But Wofa Sarpong beat me to my plan. Before I could begin to hatch a plot to escape, he'd fitted his donkey to the cart—piled with kola nuts—and ordered Kwesi to carry me on to the cart. Aminah threw me a branch and told me to chew its leaves to put on my body, to help with the soreness from the whipping. For a second, I thought of begging Wofa Sarpong to turn the cart around to let me stay with Aminah. But when I saw how the man's shoulders were hunched up and how he was furiously hitting the donkey with the same swish that had caned me, shouting, "Ko! Ko!", part of me was relieved he was taking me away.

The cart rumbled over stones and, a few times, I thought we would topple over. The forest grew denser the more we travelled, and I had to catch my breath. If only I could have fled with Aminah.

We arrived at a small hut in the middle of a palm-tree enclosure. We'd barely stopped when a tall man stooped out of the door.

"Dogo," said Wofa Sarpong.

"Wofa, you're here too early," said the tall man.

"This one's ears are too hard. She will cause me only problems. Just take her."

"I have nothing to trade here. Some salt, maybe."

"I'll take it."

Wofa Sarpong got down from the cart, dragging me down by the ears, and I almost fell, but made sure I caught myself and stood tall. I wanted to spit in his face, but he was sure to hit me and my body was too sore. The enclosure smelt like water that had stayed too long in a pot. A hen clucked by the entrance to the hut, trailed by her chicks.

"Give me the chicken, too," said Wofa Sarpong.

"I need them for eggs."

"Massa, I bring you good money and you talk about eggs."

Another chicken came out, a grey and green rooster strutting proudly, unaware it was going to end up in Wofa Sarpong's evil clutches. I looked at Dogo, the tall man, who also understood this and shrugged before following the birds around. The birds squawked and clucked, and Dogo stood up many times, fruitless, wiping his brow. Meanwhile, Wofa Sarpong went into Dogo's hut and came out with bales of cloth and some rusted farm tools.

"The cloth is not for me," said Dogo, palming one hand in the other to beg Wofa Sarpong.

"Tell the person to come to see me," said Wofa Sarpong, striding like the rooster he was about to take.

"Please," continued Dogo, but Wofa Sarpong glared at him and the tall man shut up.

I wanted to laugh, marvelling at how such a tall man could quake when small Wofa Sarpong spoke. Dogo was letting Wofa Sarpong do whatever he wanted, which meant either Dogo owed Wofa Sarpong something or the tall man wasn't very smart.

"Come and take the kola," said Wofa Sarpong, as if he were talking to one of his children.

The chickens were still roaming.

The man went into his hut and returned with three deep baskets.

"Hey, you," Wofa Sarpong said.

I didn't flinch. I took my time and then regarded him. "Hassana."

"Come and take the kola."

I took a basket, filling it with pods of kola from the cart. From the corner of my eye, I saw Wofa Sarpong chasing after the rooster. He lunged after it and fell flat. I couldn't help it. I chortled.

He eventually caught the rooster and hen and put them in the cart with the cloth, farm tools and a bag of salt.

"You still have the chicks," said Wofa Sarpong. "They will grow and give you eggs. As for this one... who will buy a hard-headed girl like this?"

"The white men in the Volta still take all kinds," said Dogo. "There is no business in the Gold Coast any more. I go east now."

"She almost let the inspector have me. Make sure the obroni takes her far far. I'll see you soon."

I hadn't wanted to learn Wofa Sarpong's language, but without even trying I could understand almost everything he said.

Wofa Sarpong climbed up into his cart and left me with Dogo, at whose feet the motherless chicks were now gathered and shivering.

Evening descended quickly, covering everything in grey.

"Come and eat," Dogo said in Hausa, one of the languages that I grew up speaking. "Tomorrow, you meet your new master."

Knowing that he could speak Hausa made me relax enough to sit down and eat the bowl of boiled beans he offered. He laid out a mat for me in the hut and spread out one outside for himself.

That night, my eyelids wouldn't close shut. Every rustle, every bird cry, every whisper of wind kept me awake. I must have fallen asleep towards the beginning of morning.

"I'll bathe first and then you'll go next," he said, sticking his head in the doorway, and waking me up.

Dogo wasn't a very smart man. No wonder Wofa Sarpong treated him as he had. Even though the night terrified me, I could easily have fled into its darkness. Now, he was leaving me on my own so he could bathe. I decided that he'd looked at me and seen a small powerless girl. I watched through the door and when he was out of sight, I rubbed the sleep out of my eyes and stole some of the beans that were sitting in the corner of his hut and tied them in a knot at the top of my cloth. Wofa Sarpong had left Dogo only three farm tools, including a small machete, which I took.

Dogo hummed and splashed water on his body, and I slid out of the hut in the opposite direction, doing what Aminah and I should have done together a long time ago. On the tip of my toes, I stepped only where I could find wet soil. I walked fast and quietly, remaining only on paths where I saw footprints, because that would lead me to people and not into a leopard's den. I walked and my stomach began to grumble. The thought of how I would prepare the beans hadn't fully formed when I'd taken them, and now raw beans weren't going to assuage my hunger. I kept going. I wanted to run as far away from Dogo as I could, then start asking for this place with blue water where Husseina had ended up.

I followed the trail and arrived at a part of the forest where palm trees had clumped together. They didn't have the mismatched look of the rest of the forest. There had to be people around. I didn't know if I could trust them, but I could trade them some beans or the machete for food and information and continue on my way. I pushed through the trees and came to an open space, not unlike Wofa Sarpong's compound. Only, here, there were also huts made of white cloth, not unlike the cloth in Husseina's dream. The similarity of it pocked the skin on my arms. I had come in with so much force that the people who lived there stopped and looked at me.

There were about five of them, all men, three of them paler than the white beans I'd stolen from Dogo. They looked just like people, with two arms and two legs, but their skin seemed to have no colour. Two men approached, one of them colourless. I couldn't imagine what they would do to me, so I held up my machete and brandished it. It bought me some time. I could turn around and run back fast to Dogo and say I got lost or I could stay and try to fight them, but they outnumbered me. Or I could reason with them.

They kept their distance, and the colourless man, probably about as old as my father, crouched. He put his hands at his sides and waved me to him. I was well and truly stuck. I had nowhere else to go, so I dropped the machete and pinched my fingers together and brought them to my lips. If they could feed me, I would find the energy to outsmart them. The colourless man seemed to have understood me and barked out something to the other man he'd come with. He wore a hat that looked like the inspector's at Wofa Sarpong's. He came and took me by the hand, and I let him. His palms were soft and made me think of a gecko's underbelly. Trust is a strange animal. I let the weight of my hands sink into his. I trusted him.

He took me to the front of a cloth hut and sat me on a mat. The hut was connected to the earth with strings and looked as if a small gust of wind could blow it over. A boy brought two calabashes—one with fingers of boiled green plantains, the other with water. I bit into the plantain, barely chewing before I swallowed. My colourless friend spoke, and a man who looked like me translated in Wofa Sarpong's language.

"What do you call yourself?"

"Hassana," I said, not even thinking that saying so could be used to return me to Dogo or Wofa Sarpong.

"Where are you going?"

What could I tell him? I didn't have the word for the colour blue. I could just say the water.

The two men exchanged words, and the interpreter tried again.

"Where's your family?"

I shook my head. I didn't feel like talking. I looked at the plantain and returned to chewing. The plantain was mostly tasteless but with a slight sweetness that made me enjoy it.

All around the village, people had come out of their huts like ants before heavy rainfall. Women and children stared at me as if I had fallen from the sky. I decided to just eat my plantain. After that I'd thank them and get going. A woman brought me another bowl. In it was nkotomire stew, the green cocoyam leaf sauce that Wofa Sarpong's wives often cooked. I only had half a finger of plantain left, so I broke it and dipped my fingers deep in the rich green sauce and slurped my fingers. I heard giggling. Children younger than me approached and were pointing at me and laughing. I bared my teeth at them and they screamed and ran to their mothers. I don't know why I did that. I dug my fingers into the nkotomire and tasted the fresh palm oil that had been used to fry the sauce, the onions that had turned golden brown, the leafiness of the nkotomire and the sharp saltiness of the dried tilapia.

"She's rude," I heard one of the mothers say and suck her teeth.

Right then, I decided to bury in my chest the fact that I could understand them. I would play dumb and use that to get fed. When I understood where I was and where I needed to go, I would escape.

I licked my fingers clean of palm oil and stew and out of nowhere a loud round burp escaped from my throat. Suddenly it hit me: I had enjoyed the meal. Either the food was well flavoured, unlike Wofa Sarpong's food, or I had begun to taste again. I stood up with the two calabashes. The colourless men had gathered by a wheel-like object that looked like the one on Wofa Sarpong's cart. Everything was strange here—the houses, the colour of the people—but I grew brave. I went to the woman who had brought over the stew and palmed my right hand in my left and lowered my knee to the ground, to show her I was grateful.

"It's all right," said the woman, taking the calabashes and waving me away.

The older colourless man came back and parted the door to his cloth hut. He put his hands together and pressed them against his cheek and closed his eyes. Sleep, he was suggesting. The last thing I wanted to do was sleep, but I did as he said and went in and lowered myself on to the mat. I hadn't taken my machete, I realized. Before I could protest, sleep fell on me and engulfed me with its warm dark fur.

We are at the waterhole, a gaggle of girls. She sits on the banks and dips her toes into the water. I duck into the water and come out, waving out to her at the shore. Come, I beckon. She shakes her shoulders up and down. Come, I insist. She refuses. We dance that way, until I wade to her and pull her into the water. At first her feet touch the pond's bed, then I drag her in deeper. She falls and flails about, struggling to breathe. She is sucked into the water and disappears.

Heavy shapes hovering over me shook me awake. I had been dreaming about Husseina, as often happened, but it wasn't her dream. Experiencing her dreams took something I hadn't yet put my finger on. I pulled myself out of my sleepy state and realized the face closest to mine was Dogo's. I almost screamed. He covered my mouth, dragged me outside the hut.

"Why did you do that?" he said to me.

I looked around and tried to catch the eye of my friend. He was staring at Dogo. What had Dogo told them? Why had I given in to sleep? That was very stupid of me.

"You can't run away just like that. You belong to me," Dogo whispered.

Maybe if I accused him of some crime, of Dogo treating me the way Wofa Sarpong had my sister, sneaking into her room, these people would understand. I opened my eyes widely at Dogo. Then again, Wofa Sarpong had tried to say we were his family and not his slaves. There must be something wrong with being someone's slave.

"No," I began. "No, no, no." I lifted my hands and covered my eyes, peeked through slits between my fingers.

"Let me take my daughter and go," said Dogo.

"I am his slave," I shouted in Wofa Sarpong's language.

To my surprise, my colourless friend—not a thin man— darted across and grabbed Dogo by the throat, lifting him up in the process. Dogo tried to say something, his voice strangled in his throat. The colourless man was also shorter than Dogo and yet the tall man was being tossed about like the dolls Husseina and I used to play with. He let Dogo go.

"Pikin dey lie," Dogo finally managed. He said it so many times it is forever etched in my mind. "She my pikin." *The child is lying*, I would later understand. *She is my child*.

"Go!" the colourless man shouted, and rained other heavy words in his language on Dogo.

Dogo stared at me before turning and leaving. His face wasn't angry, but marked with disbelief and sadness at what I'd just done. My heart felt like someone had wrung it. The wrong man was paying for the crime. It shouldn't have been Dogo in the colourless man's clasp—it should have been Wofa Sarpong. It should have been the men who had burnt my village down and killed half my family. But, I told myself, for associating with Wofa Sarpong, Dogo deserved to lose me.

I learnt that the man who had become my protector was called Richard Burtt. He gave me my own cloth hut and refused to let me have my machete back, but I knew he would strangle a man to save my life. From that day, everywhere he went, I followed. We ate together from the same plate, which I insisted on, because I didn't want to be poisoned by the village people who looked at me suspiciously. Soon, I realized people in the village also needed Richard—his presence kept them safe—so they generally left me alone.

Every night, I went to sleep in my cloth hut—tent, Richard corrected me—I willed Husseina's dream to return. I wanted to close my eyes and get lost in the world of her dreams. I would shut my eyes tight, clench my jaw, draw my knees into my chest and wait for sleep to come with its shrouding power. When it did eventually come, it would loosen my tight hug, and slow my breathing, lulling me into its warm embrace, but the dreams that came weren't her dreams—they were dreams that spoke of the past.

I would wake up, sometimes in the middle of the night, and go out of my tent. Every night, there was a different person guarding the village. Never one of Richard's people. Always people with the same skin as me. Richard told me that people with my skin were called "black people" and the people with colourless skin were called "white people". I didn't agree, since my skin was more red than black, and the people in this part of Kintampo were a deep brown. As for the ones we called white, I thought they were pink. When I told him, he laughed.

I was learning things from Richard that I was sure would make it easier to find Husseina. Richard had been in what he called "the Gold Coast" to study plants to find out what could be used to treat sicknesses. He was going to put everything he found in a book, and when I followed him around, I would hold a box with compartments in which he would throw samples of leaves. I learnt the names in Twi of plants and names Richard said were scientific. Names in English, in his language. He helped me plant my beans, which, in just a few days, sprouted into seedlings. I felt as if I had given birth to life. He'd left his wife and two daughters in a land called Great Britain to do service for his country. It was a noble thing he was doing, to willingly be separated from his family. I hadn't gone away from Aminah in the same way—I just had to find Husseina.

During afternoon sleep, a time when the whole compound went silent, I often stayed up, looking at the line that formed from the coming together of the two pieces of cloth that made my tent, or I would go outside and look at my bean plants. Then, I would memorize everything I'd learnt, repeating words so they would roll off my tongue as if I'd been born with them.

"It's not right," a woman said to me, one such afternoon, as I was touching the first pod that had grown on my plant. She was called Ma'Adjoa and had fed me on my first day there.

"You are a girl; he's a man. You're leaving yourself exposed for bad things to happen. Come and stay with me."

The little ones often sang that Ma'Adjoa had eaten the children in her womb. I was scared that what they said was true, but I felt for her. It didn't feel right for one person to be condemned by the whole village, so to thank her, I ate lunch with her and dinner with Richard. But I still slept in my tent.

About three full moons since being adopted by Richard, I was sitting outside the tent. Richard had scribbled letters in the sand. He took the stick he used when he went into the forest to search for plants and pointed at the first letter, C.

"K," I sounded.

To the next, I said, "Ah", and finally, "T."

"Put it together," said Richard.

"Cat."

He wrote another word. I struggled with it, but I could read "dog" and "ant".

Richard dropped his cane and clapped loudly, grabbed me into the air and said, "Clever girl!"

I felt so proud of myself. And yet I didn't have any idea of what I'd read.

"We have to get you books from Accra," he said. "I'll tell the next chap who comes up."

I liked learning Richard's English. Porters brought over the books Richard had ordered for me. The books were made of a very fragile kind of cloth. The first time I touched one of them, I pulled too hard and it tore.

"Treat it like an egg," said Richard.

I listened to him and grew protective of the books, like a mother hen, to the point that when the other village children came and tried to touch the books, I hit their fingers with Richard's cane. If I was not delicate, how much more so would these illiterate children be? Richard called me "the prefect of books".

Kwasidas, Sundays, became my favourite days. There was another white man we called Osofopapa, and who Richard called a priest, who went around in the mornings ringing an upside-down metal cup to get the children and the adults to join in with them. The first time I attended, I went because Richard said I would learn about a God who is good.

"Who is your God?" I asked him.

"The creator of all life. He is the reason we have breath, why there are animals and plants and rivers and forests. He's here and there and everywhere."

His God and Otienu seemed similar. I wanted to ask Otienu a lot of questions about why he let such bad things happen to my family, but I was sure we left Otienu behind in Botu, and that's where he differed with Richard's God—he wasn't here and there and everywhere. I wanted to know if this good God could answer my questions.

That first day, Osofopapa brought out a thick book, thicker than any of the ones Richard had given me, and he spoke mostly Twi, so some parts of the story remained unclear. I learnt that before the world began, it had no colour, sound, taste, form or smell. It was all darkness until their God said, "Let there be light." Then from soil he made people. The message didn't speak to me and I almost didn't go back the second Kwasida, because we didn't even get to ask questions of Osofopapa. And I could just ask Richard, who wasn't as strict-looking as Osofopapa, with his white collar and white hair. But it was good I went—it was as if Osofopapa knew he needed to find a story to keep me interested. At first, he started talking about ntaafuo and I didn't know what he meant until he said a woman called Rebecca had two babies pushing for space in one belly. I wished then that my Twi were better, so I could understand the whole story. The two boys would become two lands. One came out red; the other was holding on to the heel of the other. Yakubu and Esau. My heart started racing. In Botu, we were the only twins I knew of. I hadn't met any twins since. When he said that they would be separated, I wanted to get up and shout: "*That's what happened to Husseina and me.*" I wanted to ask: "*Did they come back together?*" I must have been making too-loud noises from my mouth because suddenly everyone was watching me. I darted my eyes left and right and stared straight at Osofopapa. They didn't know how important this was.

"The brothers would always fight," said Osofopapa. "Their lands would be at war with each other."

We fought sometimes, but that was not our relationship. I protected Husseina.

Our grandmother said I came out first, yelling so much that they had to cover my mouth. She said they were going to prepare the herbs to clean out Na, but just before they started the process of boiling hot water, another baby plopped out. She was so quiet they thought she wasn't alive. Only when my grandmother pinched her did she let out a small cry.

"Where is the place with the blue water?" I asked Richard, after the sermon with the twins.

"Water that is blue?" He shook his head.

"It has tall palm trees and water that looks as blue as the sky. There's maybe more water than land."

"Certainly not Accra. The water there is not one bit blue. You are a curious one. Where did you get such an image from? From one of your books?"

I shook my head. "My twin sister is there."

Richard's eyes widened. He regarded me as if I had turned into the madman who came here to get the white man's water.

"Like Yakubu and Esau," I said. "I have a ntaa."

"Ah," said Richard.

"I'm going to find her."

Richard laughed from his belly, which he held, then he said what he'd been thinking all along.

"You've gone mad. So many places have water and coconut trees."

"Like where?"

I remember not blinking. There was nothing he could say to change my mind. Either he helped me or I'd make my way to a place with coconut trees myself.

He asked me to tell him more about Husseina and how we were separated.

"Slavery was already illegal here in the Gold Coast. So she most likely went down the Volta and then to the coast," said Richard. "If what you say is not some crazy make-believe story, I am going down to the Basel Mission to do some work in the Volta—it might get you closer to the coast."

"Yes." I nodded.

CHAPTER THREE

Husseina

The morning was humid, and Husseina's thin wrapper clung to her body as she sat in front of Baba Kaseko's house, watching a parade of women decked in frilly white blouses and thick full skirts dance and sing. A shy sun peeked over the houses of Bamgbose Street, as if just biding its time before unleashing its heat on the attendants of the procession. Husseina clapped despite herself. Their music seeped into her bones. It was so beautiful. It reminded her of the caravans that arrived in her village, except this one contained only people dressed in shiny clothes and no animals. Also, these people weren't just passing through. They were here to be seen. They swayed left and right, pushing into a crowd that swelled further up the street they climbed. People had come out of their homes, just as she had, and those with ile petesi, two-storey houses, leant out of their upstairs windows to wave at the procession. The colours of the skirts were splendid. Bright silvers and gold, pinks and blues, a rainbow burst. Behind them, drummers rapped at the skins of their drums, producing the deepest music she'd ever heard. They seemed to be heading towards Campos

Square, a place she passed by on her way to Agarawu market. Husseina wished she could follow the procession, but didn't want to get into trouble with Baba Kaseko, so she just sat and watched. What she would give to be able to dance like the girls. To be dressed in such colours, to be free.

Drums pound, hollow out, boom again, and call to her. Their beat grows to a steady thrumming and fills her head. All her thoughts are one with the music of the drums. As if the drums are a voice calling out, "Come." Carried by the voice that is at once in her and about her, she floats to the drum song, as if on air. The music controls her limbs. She seems to be the only person around the drums. Her body absorbs the heat of the music, spinning as its volume increases and slowing down when the beat changes pace. Her body spins. And she feels, at last, free. Free of the fear that has always followed her. Fear that has chosen her. Fear that often clips her tongue and leaves her struggling to find the right words, that often leaves her in tears. Fear that is so suffocating that even now, as she rises above it, she can't completely rid herself of it. The music makes her fear keep its distance, but she isn't able to will it away for good—she is only keeping it at bay. This fear has been her constant companion. But for the first time, she feels a small tear between herself and this thing that has ruled all the years she's known. She wants to leap up to the skies, finally armed with a way of ridding herself of it, even if only temporarily. The beat slows and she spins slower. Her chest grows its own raspy music. She breathes heavily and falls.

She woke up surrounded by a flurry of white cotton. She wasn't alone in the room. She hadn't even realized she'd floated into a room. Long flowing skirts light as feathers fluttered by her and one stopped, lowered down and settled at her feet. Then she was staring into the wide, small-chinned face of a woman who looked as old as her grandmother. It was the face of love, with a crisp white scarf wrapped above it. She was the woman Husseina had seen leading the procession. Humming, the woman took a wet cloth and pressed it to Husseina's brow. The drumming had stopped. Husseina, from the corner of her eye, saw that others had befallen similar spells, and they, too, were being nursed by other women in white.

"Yemanjá's child," whispered the woman, drawing Husseina to her chest and enveloping her in a warm hug. "Yemanjá doesn't choose many people."

Husseina didn't want her to let go. It was an embrace that gave her hope.

Someone in the room said, "She's one of Baba Kaseko's erú. Must be strong to be here. He's a wicked man."

Strong wasn't a word anyone had ever used to describe her. Loyal, maybe. Reserved, definitely. Strong was a word she'd heard applied to her twin sister's fearlessness, and for her mother, who bore everything that came her way while keeping headstrong. And yet she'd always suspected that she *was* strong. Maybe a different kind of strong. After all, when evil horsemen had separated her and Hassana after they had been travelling together in a human caravan, she didn't cry. It had felt as if the shade had been taken away and Husseina had found herself under the sun on an especially hot day. And yet, as the days wore on, and as the image of her sister grew smaller and smaller, she began to accept what life had thrown her way. This, she decided, was a chance for her to bloom. So, she went where her captors told her to go, burying the horrors she and her family had suffered into her mind's reaches, and telling herself to try not to cry. And she didn't cry when she ended up in the Salaga market and when Baba Kaseko pointed to her and five others and took them down a fast-flowing river, where sometimes water elephants swam close to their boat. And when they had to walk for days upon days, carrying baskets filled with kola nuts. Nor when she arrived, disorientated and feet cracked, in the town of Lagos, where Baba Kaseko had built his large home. Lagos was to be her final destination. He had sold most of his other slaves as he had his kola nuts. She was the last one. She was to be Baba Kaseko's slave. She woke up every day, found her voice to sing, and forced herself to learn the language of Baba Kaseko and his family, forced herself to do everything asked of her, even when Baba Kaseko welted her body with his lashes.

Realizing where she was, she got up and fled to Baba Kaseko's house before anyone noticed she hadn't been sent on an errand and was missing.

Once again, she was filled with the music of the drums. Three moons had gone by since the first time it had happened and she avoided walking by the house any time she heard the first thump of a drum.

What she didn't know was that her song hadn't played in all that time.

She was deep in the bowels of Baba Kaseko's house, cleaning the room where baths were taken, acrid with the stench of urine, when the drums once again called out to her. She floated to the drums, and woke up again surrounded by white.

"Yemanjá's child has come back," said the grandmother-like lady. She pulled back from the hug and stared deep into Husseina's eyes. "Yemanjá sent you back to me. Poor child, you have to stay with that joke of an Egba man. I'm Yaya Silvina. You like Baba Kaseko? Do you want to come and stay with me? You will be free here."

Husseina wanted to shake her head no to the first question, and yes to the second, but she wasn't sure how it would look—they might think she was saying no if she shook her head first, so she just threw her body against the old lady and let the woman fold her in another hug.

The old lady winced, peeled her knees off the floor, and got up using another woman's body as support. She stretched her fingers for Husseina, and they went out of the house, Husseina seeing details she'd missed when the music had lulled her in. The entryway was lined with many pots of plants, and the compound's ground was not sandy like in Baba Kaseko's, but hard and green and laid in shapes that made Husseina feel like jumping from one to the next. They stepped out of the doorway and turned left. Husseina was pleased that Yaya Silvina wasn't wasting time. It was impossible not to compare Yaya's house with Baba Kaseko's. Yaya's ile petesi looked like two houses had been stacked on each other and stood tall and proud next to Baba Kaseko's one-storey house. His door was falling apart, and where Yaya's had been painted bright white, Baba Kaseko's had never seen a brush of paint. Husseina used to think Baba Kaseko's house was big. Not any more.

Yaya clapped her hands loudly, to announce her presence.

Baba Kaseko's eldest daughter came out, holding a metal basin of tomatoes, and on seeing Yaya, lowered the basin to the ground and curtsied.

Husseina hid behind Yaya, her heart racing.

"Call your father," said Yaya.

Not a minute had gone by and Baba Kaseko shuffled out of his room, tightening the string of his off-white shokoto below his flat belly, and wiping the crust of sleep from his eyes. That man loved to sleep! He could sleep three times a day. He was at least two heads taller than Yaya, who was barely keeping Husseina covered.

"The girl stays with me now," said Yaya.

Baba Kaseko locked eyes with Husseina. The veins in his eyes seemed to multiply, but he said nothing. The longer they stood there, the more Husseina grew worried the man would get his whip and set it on both Yaya and herself.

"This one, she's a person, not a kola nut," said Yaya.

"What?"

"Lawyer Forsythe is my good friend. He doesn't lose cases and the girl is ready to speak out against you. She will take you to slave court."

The man turned around and left without saying a word. Husseina was shocked. She'd expected a slanging match, the way people went at it in the market. She'd expected Baba Kaseko to drag her in and tell Yaya Silvina to get out of his sight. Why had it been so easy?

Or so Husseina and Yaya had thought.

But before the trouble with Baba Kaseko started, Yaya had plenty to do with Husseina. Before people could question who Husseina was, Yaya got her baptized in the stone church down Bamgbose Street. She was going to be called Vitória. Yaya said the faster Husseina learnt a trade, the faster she could learn how to be free. Yaya said it wasn't an easy thing to do after having someone tell you when to eat, sleep and breathe. Yaya knew this because she had also been enslaved, in a land called Bahia.

Husseina started learning how to sew like Yaya and learning a new religion, Candomblé, and its new Gods, orixás. She was a daughter of the house, a house full of novelties. The big table, wide enough to seat about ten people around it and with chairs that supported the back, was new to Husseina. In Botu, and even in Baba Kaseko's house, everyone sat on stools or on the floor and around a large bowl to eat in the courtyard. In Yaya's house, the first time she'd had to eat from her own bowl, she hadn't known how to begin. Yaya's adopted daughter, Tereza, was about to tuck into her bowl of eba and egusi stew, and held in her fingers a tool that reminded her of an egg. She wondered why they didn't use their hands like everybody else, and as if Tereza could see Husseina's struggle, she said, "Make as if you are going to dig the earth to plant seeds." Husseina learnt fast, and soon relished that she didn't have to soil her hands when she ate.

The space of the rooms was new. There was the small, plant-filled courtyard, when one walked in through the front door, which seemed merely decorative as most of the living was done inside. Husseina was used to living outside and only going inside to sleep. Downstairs, across from the room in which they ate, was the big hall where ceremonies were held. Yaya held a ceremony almost every week, on Saturdays. Husseina cleaned the room before and after ceremonies, and was learning the ceremonial songs—at least to hum them. She had to empty plates that had been left in various corners for the different orixás, a task she didn't quite enjoy, because she worried about doing something wrong or to offend them. There was a small room next to the ceremony room that Husseina wasn't allowed into. It was where the orixás' clothes were kept. She loved that moment in the ceremony when people who had received an orixá went away to get dressed and came out and danced as the orixá. She wondered what it would feel like to be chosen by the Gods.

The next room, to the right of the courtyard, was for receiving visitors, and the last room in the back was the kitchen. The bathroom was inside the house, not outside. And Yaya Silvina had given Husseina her own room, on the second storey. It had a raised bed, which Husseina sank into. It felt as if she'd flown into the sky and fallen asleep on a thick cloud. The same bed was invaded with small red ants only a few nights after she'd moved into the house. She threw herself on to the bed, and suddenly felt as if her skin was being pocked with a thousand needles. Tereza had helped her beat out her mattress, and Yaya admonished her for taking food to the bed. She hadn't eaten anything in the bed.

The ants didn't stop her from loving her room. Also in it was a big window that overlooked Bamgbose Street. She loved sticking her forehead on its glass pane and watching women and men come and go. Sometimes, there were people like Baba Kaseko in simple cloths draped over their shoulders; sometimes, there was a white man, dressed in what looked like three layers of clothes; then women either all in white like Yaya or similar to the way Husseina dressed when she was back in Botu, with a square of cloth wrapped around her body. There were animals, too. She liked the horses attached to carts waiting for their owners. The pigs were funny. They reminded her of people, the way the little ones chased after their mothers to get her milk, and how their mothers, exhausted, would sometimes shoo them away. The window at Yaya's was a gift. In the early evening, before she had to go and help with dinner, she watched people light up their lanterns as they prepared to sell their evening food, and how the street was lit up with huge candle-like posts that brought a daytime glow to the night. She watched how people returned from their days at work, some of them already drunk as they made their way home, especially the one they called Ship Master—he always limped home. Then there were women who began to leave their homes just as everyone else was coming home. Sometimes, Tereza watched with her, filling in the blanks that had crossed Husseina's mind. Tereza had told her those were women of the night.

"You want to know what they do," said Tereza, the whites of her eyes sparkling.

Husseina nodded.

"I'll tell you when you're old enough." Tereza laughed and smacked her thigh.

Tereza was talkative and loud, so Husseina was sure that one day she would slip up and then Husseina would learn. She could stare out of the window for hours, but often, just as she got sucked into a story, Yaya called her to come to pin some hems.

Husseina scrambled after Yaya as they wound around the Agarawu market, early one Saturday morning. She'd been living with Yaya for a month. Husseina knew Agarawu market well, because Baba Kaseko often sent her to buy tree bark or some foul-smelling concoction. Sometimes, just as she arrived at the house, another basket would be thrust at her to get more items for the house. Husseina always went without complaining, even though it was quite a long walk. In the market, no one paid attention to her, so she was happy to go back and watch the range of goods, dead and alive, being sold. Cages of birds—green, yellow, all colours. The gnarled dried hands of dead monkeys and rodents, small and large. Some other things it was impossible to identify. If Lagos was the smell of earth before it rained, in Agarawu market, that smell disappeared, buried under the stench of animals, rotting vegetables and sweat.

Yaya Silvina, dressed in white with a white scarf around her head, waved here, paused there to say hello, and they roamed the entire market before stopping in front of a mat covered with a motley of fabrics that glimmered in the morning sun. She held on to Husseina, also dressed in white, and knelt down, and began to pick and rub the fabric between her fingers. She picked up one bale, as blue as the sky, and held it up against the sun. The halo of the sun was clear from where Husseina sat—it was too transparent. No one had come yet to see to them, so Yaya continued choosing different pieces of fabric and holding them up against the sun, until she found a green fabric opaque enough to block the sun's rays. Then, she picked another that barely held away the sun, one that could have been the sun itself with its golden shine. Yaya went for a range of green and gold fabrics. She looked around—still no one had shown up.

"Where's that one?" said Yaya, with her tendency to switch to Portuguese when irritated.

They stood up and scanned the market with its flower-garden display of umbrellas. Husseina especially loved the sound of this place. The voices of a thousand people trying to get a good deal, and many more trying to peddle their wares. The beats of distant drumming. The bleats of sheep and goats, probably trussed up, waiting to be sold as meat. Loud singing, most likely from someone whose brain got tired of living in this reality and had found a new place to live in.

A small body ran towards them, clutching a piece of cloth, and when he arrived, he wasn't that small. He towered over Husseina and Yaya, even as he doubled over to catch his breath.

"Good day, Yaya," he said, between gasps for air. "Someone tried to steal my cotton." He brandished the small square of fabric.

"I almost went to your rival," said Yaya. "For this small piece, you almost lost your customer."

"Oh! Don't say that."

Yaya extracted the two fabrics she'd chosen and showed them to the seller.

"From Brazil?" she asked.

"You shouldn't be asking. Certified Brazilian."

"I'll give you one pound."

"Bring on your money."

They went on and on, Yaya proposing a price and the trader trying to increase it, until the trader relented and took Yaya's coins.

Yaya hooked her arm in Husseina's and they continued to a woman who sold calabashes full of buttons. Yaya bent over and grabbed a handful of buttons, thread and beads. Yaya's client—a Brazilian woman marrying a Saro lawyer—wanted a wedding that would outshine all other Lagos weddings. The Saros had come from a place called Sierra Leone, and Tereza told Husseina there was often competition between their community and the Saros. The woman wanted her in-laws to know that the Brazilians could not be outdone.

When they got home, Yaya pushed through the door with her fabric. Husseina followed with a basket of beads and buttons. As she was about to close the door, something thumped to the ground just outside the entrance. It was a rodent, a rat or squirrel, dried like the ones she'd seen in the market. It looked rock hard and its smell of death wafted up. She wanted to kick it away from their threshold, but its bloodied claws stuck out, as if it had been scratching at something before it was killed. Probably better not to touch it. Had someone thrown it at them? She looked up, and a few people were walking away in the direction of Campos Square. Not one of them looked back. She shut the door, wondering if she should tell Yaya about it.

"Vitória!" Yaya shouted. "We have work to do."

Lagos had its share of rats, but for one to just fall from the sky was strange. Maybe it wasn't important, she convinced herself, although she had a hunch it might be—but, sometimes, it was easier not to talk. The creature may simply have got stuck in the space between the door and the frame. Yaya had more pressing things to deal with than a dead rat.

The next two weeks were spent cutting, stitching, trimming, hemming, ruching and sewing outfits for the wedding and for some of the guests. Husseina marvelled at the machine that Yaya used to stitch. She could make a whole dress in less than three hours with the thing. She thought of her father and how, with a machine like this, he could have produced at least ten shoes in the time it took him to make one. Where *was* Baba? Where was her mother? Where were her siblings? Where was her twin? She would not give in to these questions. Instead, she filled her days with as much activity and window-watching as she could, because she was sure there was no easy answer to any of these questions. Luckily, there was so much to do, and she didn't spiral into her thoughts of loss.

Two days before the wedding, Yaya's dining room was overtaken with bodies trying on their gowns. Husseina watched them, reflecting on how different these women were. Some of them threw off their clothes in front of everyone; others hid themselves in corners to delicately peel off their clothes. They all spoke Portuguese freely and yet some of them were as dark as night; some were like her sister Hassana's red; others were the light colour of shea butter. She found each of them beautiful as she sat on the floor, watching them parade in front of Yaya after they'd put on their clothes. The ones who'd easily thrown off their clothes strutted back and forth like male guinea fowl, with their chests out. The quieter girls looked at their feet. She knew she was like these quiet women, and while she understood their shyness, seeing it from the other side made her uncomfortable. She wanted to tell them to be bolder, that they too were beautiful—no less so than their bold sisters.

Suddenly, one of them shrieked, setting off all the other girls. Everyone hopped from one foot to the other, as if the ground were made of crocodiles, and Husseina hopped, too, her body pocking over in fear, her old friend. They all rushed to the corner of the dining room and the one who had screamed pointed. A black and gold python curled in on itself on her dress. It was at once bewitching and frightening and, at first, it seemed harmless. Then it uncurled itself and wagged its tail. The snake raised its head, its forked tongue sliding in and out of its grey mouth, as it started to glide forward towards the girls. One of the girls screamed again, and fear gripped Husseina's belly and legs.

"Everyone, to the ceremony room," Yaya said and repeated in Portuguese.

The girls fled to the narrow doorway, pushing themselves through and screaming. A few of them scraped elbows and arms in the scramble. She looked back and the creature had moved to the wall. How had it come in?

Yaya closed the door between the two rooms and sent Tereza to get one of the drummers who lived down Bamgbose Street to come and remove the snake. The girls kept rubbing their arms and shaking their bodies, as if the snake had crept over them. Husseina remembered that her father had said that snakes were their family's symbol, so he didn't make shoes out of their skin. Snakes were supposed to be protective of their family, but now she felt only fear. She, like the other girls, wanted the snake gone.

Even though Yaya told him to take the creature out without killing it, the drummer came armed with a sharp shovel and said it could have been there because of bad medicine. When he opened the door, Husseina pushed her way to the front. She didn't understand why she was both attracted to and repelled by the creature. When she saw the drummer thrust down his shovel at the snake's head, she closed her eyes. As she opened them, the snake's body uncoiled and coiled back in a circle. The drummer thrust his shovel at the head again, his back covered in beads of sweat. The snake stopped moving, and the drummer picked up the body and asked for a basket to take it out. Yaya sent Husseina to the kitchen.

"It could have been good meat," he said, when she handed him the basket.

"Why isn't it good meat any more?" Husseina asked, following him.

"You don't eat bad juju. Anyone using pythons is doing powerful medicine."

"What would it have done to us?"

"Bitten you or strangled you to death. It could have changed into a person."

Husseina shivered. Who would it have changed into? They had experienced such warm, amusing moments only minutes before the snake made its appearance. It made her itch with annoyance how life was never steady. Good times never seemed to last.

As much as Husseina enjoyed staring out of her window, she looked forward to the ceremonies in Yaya's house even more. Mostly because the food was rich. There were boiled eggs and stewed chicken, but also people were always nice when they came to the temple. She'd never met anyone who wore a squeezed face during a ceremony and yet there were people whose lives were not easy, Tereza had told her. One woman had lost many babies. Another man's home flooded every time the rains came. Despite these things, they seemed to smile the brightest during the ceremonies. When Husseina asked why, Tereza said it was the axé, the life force, of the temple and of Candomblé. Life was allowed to just *be*.

One evening, one of the attendants walked in with a smelly male goat just before the ceremony began, and Yaya asked Husseina not to come into the ceremony hall. Instead, she sat outside, a thing she hadn't done since moving into Yaya's home, and watched the people of Bamgbose Street come and go. It was different watching them from her window and being at the same level with them down on the stoop. Upstairs, she almost felt invincible. She could spit on someone's head and they wouldn't even realize it. Down here, she tried to be as invisible as she could. A mother and her children hurried by, the children in scraps of clothing. Then a herd of cattle loitered on the street, their long horns hitting each other, some of them white, others spotted black and white. They took their time to leave the street, so much so that they didn't leave her room to notice who was standing behind them. Husseina gasped. Why had she been foolish?

"As my people say, every day for the thief, one day for the master," he said, coming closer till he towered over her.

Husseina wanted to scream, but fear clamped her mouth shut. As if Baba Kaseko knew she would scream, he put his leathery fingers over her mouth.

"Tell your old lady that more is coming her way. You don't steal from Baba Kaseko just like that. You are all going to fall sick. You'll be fine one minute; the next you will hold your belly. Next time, think before you cross me. Tell that Aguda woman of yours. She took my property and expects me to forget? I've sent things you can see—those were your warnings. What I have for you now will take you by surprise."

Then it hit Husseina: the ants, the rat, the snake, they were all Baba Kaseko's medicine. She got up and ran inside, burst into the ceremony room without thinking—just then, the drummer who had killed the snake was running a knife across the goat's neck. He slit the furry neck, and out of it burst bubbles of blood. The creature screeched so loudly, Husseina thought it was a person. Yaya Silvina stood up and began singing. Husseina shut the door loudly and ran upstairs. She checked her bed to make sure it was ant-free. She slid under her cover cloth. The day was like a nightmare with no escape. She curled herself into a ball. Back in Botu, when her father disappeared, a sacrifice was held for him, but she hadn't attended it, because children weren't allowed to partake in them. She was glad they'd kept her away because she wasn't ready for any of that.

Husseina's thoughts were racing. Was she in trouble for seeing the sacrifice? How would she bring up Baba Kaseko to Yaya? Would she have to go back to him? Otherwise what would he do next? There was no way Husseina wanted to go back to him. She would rather stay with Yaya and take whatever Baba Kaseko sent their way. She was sure Yaya was powerful, especially after the scene she'd just witnessed.

Heavy thuds on the landing stopped her thoughts. Yaya opened the door and shuffled in. She sank her hips on to Husseina's bed.

"*Am I in trouble?*" she wanted to blurt out, but the words didn't want to leave her mouth.

"I told you not to come inside," Yaya said, searching Husseina's eyes.

"The snake was Baba Kaseko's," Husseina said. "He said he will hurt us even more for crossing him. Yaya, his eyes were red. Maybe he was the snake that came in here."

"If he was the snake, he would be dead by now," said Yaya. "But I should have known he'd sent it."

"Maybe his spirit left the snake's body before the drummer killed it. Yaya, everything he's sent has involved pain or death. The ants... The rat was dead. The snake died. He said we'd fall sick."

"Tell me everything he said again."

Husseina did as told, then she said, "He said what he's sending next, we wouldn't be able to see."

The old woman said, "I'm going to Bahia. I was going to leave you here and go and come back, but it's not safe. It's better if I take you to Bahia."

She didn't know what Bahia was, or what it would bring, but her heart swelled with impatient excitement. Anything to get away from that fearsome Baba Kaseko.

"To prepare you, from now on, Tereza is going to speak to you only in Portuguese," said Yaya.

*

Husseina was glad to have Tereza teach her Portuguese. Tereza wasn't serious like Yaya, and Husseina could ask her questions. There was an unspoken rule in Botu that children didn't talk back to elders, and in Lagos, it was the same. Tereza was more like an older sister. She explained that once Husseina went away, she would become an Aguda like her. One who was taken away from home. Husseina wanted to retort that, in that case, she was already an Aguda, but she pressed her tongue between the blades of her teeth. Tereza said that Yaya was required by the British law of Lagos to have Husseina take English classes, but instead Yaya was sending her to Bahia because being able to receive Yemanjá was more valuable than knowing how to speak English. Tereza confessed to Husseina that she wanted to start a business selling goods between the Gold Coast and Lagos and was not really interested in continuing ceremonies while Yaya was away, but warned Husseina to keep this to herself. Husseina was glad to be confided in, but she also understood the keeping of secrets. She herself hadn't told anyone about Hassana, because she didn't want them treating her differently. After about a year of living in Lagos, she'd learnt that twins were revered—because of this, she was sure that if Yaya knew, she would tell her to go and look for her sister.

Yaya asked Husseina to dress in her sharpest gown and the two of them walked towards Campos Square and made their way down to a place called Marina. In all this time, Husseina knew they were close to water, especially when the rains came and people's homes flooded. She just hadn't realized they were completely surrounded by water. In the caravan heading to the Salaga market, there'd been a lot of talk of the big water, and then when Baba Kaseko had bought her, they'd travelled on what she thought was the big water, but from what Yaya had told Husseina, the big water was still ahead of her. It was what they would cross to get to Bahia. It seemed menacing. If there was one thing that made her clutch to her fear, it was deep and wide water. She wanted to go to Bahia with Yaya, but didn't want to have to cross water.

They marched up a street with even bigger houses than on Bamgbose Street. These must have been six rooms wide and went up to four storeys. They passed by a box of a building, as white as Yaya's clothing, then another that was smaller but coloured like a pale brown bean, and then a string of three identical blocks, until Yaya stopped and took a look at Husseina. Yaya dipped her finger in her mouth, and used the wet finger to wipe Husseina's cheeks.

"Let's go over the story again," she said.

Husseina was Yaya Silvina's niece, who had come from Ikere after she lost her mother. Her father went missing when she was a girl—at which point Yaya Silvina would suggest that, like her, he'd probably been sent over the big water, and when Yaya Silvina finally made it back to her village, Husseina was one of the only relatives still around.

The British authorities didn't question their story and issued Husseina with a passport—a paper with her name, Vitória Silvina, and a picture of the Queen of England, sealed with a stamp.

Before they left for Bahia, a ceremony was held for Yemanjá, orixá of the waters, for safe passage.

The drums sing the same song. A call to come to them. She is overtaken, filled with their song, and her body shakes with their beat. Their music sends her body forwards and backwards, raises her limbs to the skies. She is free. She whirls, as if being pulled downwards, and then she rises. She is a spiral that never ends. She can do anything. She is ready for her journey.

Yaya Silvina warned that the journey would be one of the hardest things Husseina would suffer. She herself had been on those seas four times. The first time was as a girl, when she was snatched from her village and put in a barracoon for what felt like many moons before being forced on to a ship. At first, she was left to play around because she was a child. But when it was discovered that the slaves were plotting to jump overboard, everybody was chained to a post or to another person. She'd spent the whole journey plastered to the bodies of two other people. Too many bodies in one small wooden space. Hundreds of children, women and men. One person she was tied to didn't make the crossing. It took days for the captain of the ship to come down and let his crew throw the body overboard. When they were allowed on the deck, they had guns constantly trained on them. Water and food were rationed. They arrived in Bahia and she was sold to a plantation owner.

It would be different for Husseina because she was going on the ship as a free person, with a British passport.

Husseina and Yaya set off early, crossed the lagoon in a canoe that Husseina had to be carried into, and arrived at the Lagos Bar, where a group of passengers had already gathered. It was a mix of brown-skinned people and some white men and women. In the distance, several large ships floated on the sea, and it astonished Husseina how these huge boats didn't sink and seemed to lightly skim the surface of the water. Husseina had refused to deal with the fact that she was going to cross water, but now, standing before the big wide-open water, she couldn't deny it any more. The lagoon was child's play.

She'd had a terrifying recurring dream as a child, probably one of the only dreams she hadn't shared with her sister. In the dream, very quickly, she was surrounded by water. It filled her throat and her lungs, bloated her and simultaneously sucked her into a vortex that spun and spun until she woke up choking. It always felt unending, and she'd told no one about the dream, because it frightened her lips shut. For days, she would walk around dazed, trying to make sense of it. It kept her out of water. It made her resent Hassana for being cavalier with water. Going down to the river with Baba Kaseko, she'd clutched his smock until they'd reached dry land. And now she had to cross this huge, unending lake.

A man sitting at a desk took their passports, examined the slip, wrote in a big book, then let them pass. Yaya Silvina climbed into a branch boat, where some of the gathered they'd seen earlier were seated. Husseina stood on the shore, rooted to the sand.

Come, beckoned Yaya.

Husseina shook her head.

"Stop being a child," chided Yaya.

After a loud sucking of his teeth, one of the rowers splashed out of the canoe to hoist her into it. She was ashamed of her fear, so she looked down at her fist resting on her thighs. Another four people joined them and the canoe's rowers, seated in the middle, pulled their oars towards their chests to get moving.

This water seemed wider, terrifying, because it was never calm; the waves crested and fell forever. Husseina looked at the land she was leaving behind, and thought of her family. She had no idea in which direction they were any more. She'd travelled so far that she was losing her language. She could say quite a lot in Portuguese, and even thought in Yoruba, while Gourmanchéma was for very specific things, which only came in snatches now. She'd left home a long time ago, and even though it wasn't a choice she'd made, she had accepted her new life and longed for what the next land would bring.

When the canoe arrived at the ship, which was enormous now that they had pulled up beside it, they had to reach up for a rope ladder, and it was so shaky Husseina clung to the roughness of the rope, fearing she would fall into the waves below, bringing her dream to life. Yaya went up ahead of her, and Husseina followed, placing both feet on one rung at a time. Her belly ached, and she held her breath, only releasing it after she was up on the deck. Aboard the ship, everything was cut from wood and long poles stuck out of the ship into the air, from which flew white squares of fabric. They were surprisingly loud, producing a sound stuck between a constant *slap* and *whoosh*. She stared and stared at the fluttering in the wind.

Yaya, unsurprised by all the newness, having been on a ship many times, prodded Husseina ahead, saying they wouldn't find a good berth if they kept lingering. They went down two flights of a narrow wooden staircase and came to a landing with several doors lining the hallway. Yaya briskly pressed her palm against the first door and it was bolted shut. She went to the next and it wasn't until the fifth door to the left of the corridor that they were able to find a free room. In it were two beds, one on top of the other, and a round window against which the waves crashed, making Husseina wonder how solid the window was. She held on to the wooden frame of the bed, because the ground on which she stood felt as if it would slip away from her at any minute.

"You'll get used to it after four days," said Yaya, taking off the sheet on the bed and shaking it out. "Make your bed."

Husseina pulled off the sheet and copied Yaya, but her head felt too heavy on her neck.

"I don't feel well."

Yaya pursed her lips and hurried Husseina out of the room. She took the key out of the lock and ushered Husseina upstairs and outside.

The damp ocean air felt better. Husseina thought about the stories Yaya had told her about the other people who had made this journey not because they wanted to, not with the comfort of a bed, with no clothes on, tied to each other, forced to lie cramped together. Her head swirled. Before she could help it, she dry-heaved and Yaya led her to the side of the ship, where all the akara she'd eaten for breakfast came out.

"If you're already sick, this is going to be a long journey," said Yaya, rubbing Husseina's back.

Husseina retched and retched, overtaken by sadness. She thought of Yaya's first trip on the sea. Who were these people who thought it was right to put human beings into such vessels and to treat them worse than animals? Surely they weren't humans themselves, to be capable of such cruelty. She had felt caged in their room, yet this, she knew, was comfort. She thought also of the people Yaya had told her about who hadn't made it. What happened to their spirits so far away from home? And what had happened to their bodies, thrown into this wide and probably deep lake?

Yaya extracted groundnuts from a cloth tied around her waist.

"One of the tricks I've learnt is don't leave your stomach empty."

Husseina was meant to sleep on the top bunk and Yaya on the bottom, but Husseina could keep nothing in her belly, so at the foot of the lower bed they kept a metal bucket that Husseina could vomit into. Yaya paid a boy, not that much older than Husseina, to come in every hour to empty the bucket into the sea.

Even when she was near sleep her stomach felt no better. Only when sleep completely took over did she have peace.

We are running from a chasing fire. It stretches its fiery arms, tries to engulf us in its heat, but together we're beating it. She is running too fast. She breaks our grip on each other. She's gone.

She spent the next two days completely emptied and didn't leave the room despite Yaya's insistence that fresh air would help her. She made do with groundnuts. When her eyes opened, all she saw was the water crashing against her window. Sometimes, the water reached the top of the window; mostly, she saw a grey spread of sky, once in a while dotted with a bird. She thought of home, of Baba, Na, Aminah, her brother, grandmother and, most of all, of the other part of herself, Hassana. Who was still alive? Who had escaped their bodies and become air? Where would they go next? Would she herself survive this? Would she see any of them again? What was this life that gave you everything and then took it all away?

On the fourth day, Yaya brought her a morsel of kola nut—red, meaty and bitter—which she chewed. Then Yaya gave her a cup of water, which she drank. Yaya helped her out of the room and outside. The world had completely changed. All around them was water and sky. No other soul. No land. No ships. It was beautiful and empty and frightening all at once. Then, a bird flew in the sky and the loneliness went away. Yaya gave Husseina a banana, and it stayed down. In the distance, a fish jumped up into the sky and went back to where it felt most at home. This was so different from the land of Botu. She wondered why she was being led on this voyage. What would be its purpose?

Strength came back to Husseina day by day. Soon, she was helping Yaya clean their room as well as the rooms of others to earn some coins here and there. She spent a lot of time on the deck, contemplating the wideness of the ocean. The fluttering of the white sails gave her days a steady beat. She watched the other travellers, some of whom had not made this trip before, and many for whom this was life, like the boy who had emptied her bucket. He lived on the ship. He came and spoke to her often. He said that when the captain had adopted him, he felt an instant kinship with him.

After about twenty-five days on the sea, Yaya roused Husseina and told her to come upstairs. Up on the deck, many of the travellers lined up on the edges, and ahead of them was a luminous sun, showing the first traces of land, a dark band beyond the water. Someone started beating a drum that lit up Husseina's heart. They had survived.

The shade of land widened, but impatience also set in. It was so close and yet so far. People went away and came back. Husseina didn't want to miss anything, but Yaya pulled her away to go and eat.

After her meal of boiled beans and gari, she went back and saw that the land was beginning to hug them. The wind speed increased and sails fluttered above them. More ships came into view. As they got closer, tall coconut trees bent and whispered words of welcome.

They made for a port filled with even more ships. Above them, land seemed to shoot from the water. It was dotted with trees and tiny boxes of houses. Husseina had never seen land so high.

Yaya pressed the small of Husseina's back. "Welcome to Bahia."

CHAPTER FOUR

Hassana

After a long four-month wait, Richard kept his word and helped me load a chest with all the books he'd gifted me and the clothes the villagers had sewn for me, and off we went to the Basel Mission.

Our path there was hemmed in by trees and hills and mountains that sometimes overshadowed the trees. On some stretches a porter carried me, and when I had to walk on my own, I had to stop and swallow as much air as I could, because I couldn't breathe properly. I towered over some of the porters, like Kwame, who I knew from bringing things to Richard from time to time. I refused to let him carry me. He and the others didn't seem to suffer from a loss of air, as Richard and I did. To make matters worse, we had to climb up the hills and walk on their ridges. It was the safest way, because in the forest dwelt leopards and other wild animals. In it, said the porters, were also people who weren't afraid of kidnapping us, even if we were accompanied by a white man. In fact, Richard's presence made us valuable targets. Up on the hill, we could supposedly see better, but all I beheld were the green, boll-like tree crowns below us. I was lucky I wasn't carrying my chest on my back and that Kwame was doing that for me. I slipped many times. Kwame told me to push my weight into my heels, but I felt off balance so often that the only solution was to get on all fours and climb up the hill like a toddler.

We arrived at a flat surface, where the trees grew sparse. I caught my breath and marvelled at how far up we had travelled. Kwame laughed and said it was a baby hill. We continued walking on a small trail and, below us, the trees appeared like green cotton. I had to admit it was beautiful. The sun hit its highest point. Richard asked for a break. We had packed fruits and boiled plantain, which Richard asked me to serve the porters, who had dropped their packages, sprinkled water on their bodies and were seated on the grass. I wondered what was going through their minds. Would these boys, some of them no older than me, carry things for the rest of their lives? It was the big lesson Aminah taught me. She said we had to keep dreaming, and once a dream became real, to make new dreams. My first dream was to find Husseina. And when we found each other, I'd dream bigger. I was beginning to read Richard's language—he said once I got better, I could even go to the big town, Accra, and work for his people.

After travelling for about three days, we arrived in Abetifi, which, to my dismay, sat in the bowl of a mountain range much higher than the one we'd come from. Did the mountains ever move and fall in on themselves? What if a strong wind came and knocked them down? I wasn't assured about this new place.

"Welcome back to Abetifi," boomed a voice, and Richard, his white shirt now stained dusty red, rushed towards another white man, who was wider, taller and bearing an impressive rectangular beard. They folded each other in a hug that made me think of two elephants colliding.

Richard waved me over and my mouth grew dry. Behind the man came a mix of black and white people, and they were all teeth. This was the first time I saw a white woman. And there were two of them. One wore yellowish hair that strangely scraped her shoulders—my hair stood up and proud and only touched my shoulders when I braided it. The other had her hair rolled into a ball, so I couldn't study it, and she looked older and dragged one of her legs. She was maybe mother to the other one. They both had breasts like my mother and sister. The woman with hair to her shoulders was slim with skin shaded almost orange. She looked unhappy. Or sad more like. The older one, who shone happiness and joy, came and placed her hands on my shoulder.

"Welcome, Hassana," she said, and I exhaled in relief.

I hadn't realized just how much I'd needed to be around women. Wofa Sarpong. Dogo… In Kintampo, except for Ma'Adjoa, the women had rejected me—mostly because I kept to myself—and even Richard had made me hold my breath. I missed my mother, grandmother and sisters.

In Richard's language, children surrounded me, singing, "Welcome, Hassana! Welcome, Hassana."

My chest burst open and I cried. I hadn't expected to. The tears just fled from my eyes. The woman holding my shoulder drew me to her and patted my back. Then she led me into the biggest house I'd ever seen.

That evening, Richard broke my heart. He said he was staying three nights then heading for Accra. When I said I would go with him, he said in Kintampo it had been fine for me to stay with him because it was a village. In Accra, it would look bad if he made me live with him. Some might call me his slave—or worse, his prostitute. I didn't know what a prostitute was. He'd said it in hushed tones. He said in Abetifi, I would be taken care of, I would learn to improve my reading and writing, and it was the best place for me. He would leave me with a Bible, to have something to remember him by. I was hurt because this seemed to have always been his plan. Even if I hadn't told him about Husseina, I grew convinced he would have brought me here. When he said goodbye, it was as if he planned to see me again, but I knew it would be the last time we'd see each other. My hand lay limp in his. That night, my sadness brought Husseina's dreams to me. I could always tell which ones were hers, because they were of places I'd never seen before.

I stand on a small mass of land surrounded by water. Water is everywhere. Below us, waves rush against the mountainside. The bones at my knees turn soft at the thought of falling. I fall, but land on my feet.

After Richard left, his friends folded me into their lives so fully that my anger with him floated away like a baby bird's feather in the breeze. My new hosts had a lot to teach me, and while I found them strange—even after spending time with Richard—I needed them on my side, so I tried not to break their rules, which was not always easy. The best way to stay out of trouble was to become like Husseina—quiet and mouse-like. They lived so differently from my people, as if we were cats and they were dogs, or the other way round. I like cats, so we were definitely the cats. Unlike in Kintampo, where Richard lived in a home that could be uprooted by a gust of wind, here it looked like they meant to stay; they had used wood and sand and stone, and built homes that stood taller than those of the locals of Abetifi. The tallest was a building they called the church, with a tower topped with a cross. Richard once told me the cross was the most important symbol for Christians because a man called Yesu died on the cross to save all humanity from going to hell. When we read the Bible—which happened here a lot more than in Kintampo—I honestly liked the stories about Yesu less. I liked the older stories, where God came to the defence of his people.

Not long after I'd arrived in Abetifi, I got into a fight with a girl because she called me a slave. I lashed out and scratched her so badly, she bled from lines I'd etched in her face. Her family came to the mission because they wanted to have me caned, but Mrs Ramseyer, the older woman, sat us all down and taught us a lesson on turning the other cheek, like Yesu said. Not to pay for pain with more pain. She talked to even the girls' parents as if they were the same age as the girl and me. As the family was getting up to return to the village, Revd Ramseyer said, his tone stern, that if I hit anyone again, I would be excluded from the mission.

I don't know if this satisfied the family and I understood them—I had hurt their daughter and needed to be punished, not lectured to. In the older part of the Bible, the God of the Israelites commanded Joshua to destroy Jericho, because the people of Jericho had sinned against God and their sin would stain his chosen people. That spoke to me. If I got my hands on the people who had broken up my family, I would want my God to destroy them in the same way, collapse their walls, burn all their houses to the ground. In Abetifi, they said we should be more like Yesu, so on Sundays, at church, they always read from Matthew, Mark, Luke and John. Mrs Ramseyer was even more taken with a person called Saul who became Paul and kept telling me I should get baptized. It meant I would become a new person, a Paul. I was happy with the way I was. I didn't understand why everyone—from Wofa Sarpong to these people—wanted me to change my name. I was happy to remain Hassana.

The other big building was the main house. At two floors, it was roomier than the church, even though the church was taller, and it was where Mrs Ramseyer and her family lived. The ceiling was high, and the walls were painted white and adorned with drawings and photographs of people I would come to learn were Mrs Ramseyer's family in a place called Switzerland. It was comforting to learn that they, too, had left home. Although it still didn't make sense to me why a person would choose to move if they weren't forced to. If I had the choice I would still be in Botu. They decided to leave their home and got on a big boat to come here just to proclaim the word of the man called Yesu and to tell us how the way we lived before would hurt our souls. It sounded like madness to me. All the same, I liked the big house. In it were books and lamps and chairs that could seat more than one person. We, the children who lived in the mission house—girls who had been brought over by people like Richard—sometimes ate meals with them there, but only when the children of Abetifi weren't around. The children of Abetifi had families they could return to on weekends and holidays. I found myself wishing that life could always be a holiday.

I didn't want to make any friends to distract me from my plan, but one day, the children from the village had surrounded Afua, a birdlike girl who barely spoke, and were teasing her for not washing. I couldn't help it—I broke into their circle, grabbed Afua's wrist and dragged her out. The children shouted that I was smelly, too, but their words bounced off me and fell to the ground. Poor Afua burst into sobs and thanked me for saving her. Afua was small, but her armpits reeked like a grown-up who hadn't washed for a few days. I told her to wash twice a day with a sponge. After that, she followed me everywhere, reminding me of Husseina. When she did talk, which was seldom, she told me bits of her story. Over time, I was able to glue together the pieces: her father had given her away because she was the sixth of nine children, and when the tenth child was born, her mother passed away. The man who had bought her had heard that missionaries were buying slave children to free them and so brought her to see Revd and Mrs Ramseyer. The reverend screamed at the man for such a preposterous suggestion, took Afua from him, and sent the man out of the Christian village with threats to send him to slave court.

The very first holiday was the Christmas of 1892, celebrating the birth of Yesu. I had been there for about three months and still hadn't been baptized because I confessed to Mrs Ramseyer that I didn't understand what it meant to be saved. She was surprisingly patient. She said I was the first person who had not just said yes. Many said yes to being baptized and went back to worshipping their idols when they left the mission. She said my honesty was good. Well, the whole truth was that I really didn't believe their stories, not in my heart.

For Yesu's birthday, they cooked a large duck, and we sat at the big table, which the family had covered with a red cloth, and we held hands and prayed, thanking God for sending his only son to come down to earth to die for our sins. The meat was dry and tasteless—the complete opposite from how juicy it had looked. Na would have taken that bird and made a stew that would have had everyone licking their fingers. Most of the bird was still there after this meal. After lunch, Mrs Ramseyer's daughter Rose, with her always-pinched face, brought out a stack of brown-paper-covered gifts, which she gave to us and told us to open the next day. I could tell it was a book, and my heart sank thinking it was another Bible—I already had a Bible.

During holidays, the family let me, Afua and the others who stayed behind sleep in the main house. Afua and I shared a room. In it, we had two beds, a desk and chair, and a painting of Yesu on the wall. He had a pale face with blue eyes and long hair like Mrs Ramseyer's. I really couldn't understand why his death saved me. We couldn't be more different.

I held the present in my arms as I drifted off to sleep and slept so deeply until I felt the presence of bodies next to me. I opened my eyes and beheld the faces of Afua, Cecile, Helene and John, the younger mission children.

"Time to open presents," they shouted and dragged me down to the sitting room.

We sat on the soft carpet on which we often read stories. I tore at the brown paper covering my present and was pleased to find it wasn't a Bible.

"It's an atlas," said Mrs Ramseyer, lowering herself to the ground to join us. "Mr Burtt thought you would like it."

She brushed her palm over a green and blue circle and said, "This is the whole world." She then pointed to the right of two circles that were joined together and said, "We are here."

There was a big map of Africa in the sitting room, with the letters *AFRIQUE*, so the shape of Africa was familiar. I just didn't know it was the land we lived on. Surrounding Africa, itself a light pink colour, was blue, which Mrs

Ramseyer called "the sea". The sea touched other lands but made up most of the earth.

As I studied the curves between the sea and the land, it hit me. If there was that much blue water in the world, Husseina could be anywhere. I didn't know whether to laugh or cry. The gift made the ground the sky; it shifted my balance and turned over my world. After that first dream, I thought I would find out about the blue waters and simply go there. I hadn't realized how big and wide the world was.

John started making a horrible noise, thumping his palm against a small drum, and his parents—other missionaries from a place called Germany—laughed. I told them I was poorly and went back to my room.

I could only sound out the letters and they made no sense to me. Why would Richard leave me a gift I could barely use? Why was the world so big?

The other pupils came back to the school in the new year, and I decided I would do everything in my power to learn how to read properly. By Easter of 1893, I could piece together longer words and make meaning of them. Then, I took out Richard's gift.

The atlas was covered in grey, with a black binding. *Letts's Complete Popular Atlas*. I opened the page of the whole world. Where we were, where Mrs Ramseyer had pointed with her finger over Christmas, wasn't even labelled as "the Gold Coast". I wondered if I would find Botu on the map and if I could make my way back there. I flipped pages till

I found a detailed map of Africa, and I spent so much time glaring at the map and sounding out letters that my eyes ached. I didn't see Abetifi marked on the map, but I saw Jenne, the last place my baba said he was going before he disappeared. Then I saw Gurma. My heart raced. I knew our Gurma people stretched beyond Botu, but it wasn't where Husseina was. I had to stay focused. Husseina had crossed the big sea and could be anywhere in the world, but not Gurma. I needed to find her. Instead I was stuck in a place where the people were only obsessed about a white man with drooping hair who died years and years ago. I screamed into my pillow.

I must have shouted too loudly, because the door cracked open slowly and Mrs Ramseyer shuffled in, her face squeezed in worry.

"What is wrong?" she asked.

I pointed at the atlas.

"It's a few years old—maybe ten years old—but most places still look like this. You don't like it?"

"It is really beautiful," I said. "It just reminded me of my troubles."

Mrs Ramseyer sat down on the bed and it creaked. "I have a lot of troubles, too. More like sadness. Sometimes, it helps to talk."

She opened up her arms and I pushed my body into her flesh.

"What makes you sad?" I asked.

"Many things. I miss my home sometimes."

"Me, too," I said.

"I am here doing God's work, and sometimes, if I close my eyes, it almost feels like home because I also grew up in a town in the mountains. But I left behind everything and came here with Fritz—Revd Ramseyer. There's no snow here. No cheese... You might say I chose to do it myself, but it doesn't take away the sadness."

"You could always go back home," I said. "I don't know where home is."

Mrs Ramseyer was quiet.

"Do you know what it's like to not choose to leave behind your family? To live like an animal in some strange person's house till they decide you are not useful to them any more? To lose part of yourself? To lose your twin?"

Mrs Ramseyer looked away from me, closed her eyes, and when she opened them, tears had filled her eyes. She took off her glasses.

"You just made my skin pock."

It's true—the woman's skin looked like chicken skin and the white hairs on her arm stood up. She rubbed her arms, as if to wipe off the pocks.

"We have a lot in common, my dear Hassana," she said, dabbing her cheeks and smearing her hands on the creases of her woollen dress. "For four years, Fritz and I were kept hostage. Do you know what that means?"

I shook my head.

"We were prisoners. We were captured and kept by the Asante. Some days, we had our hands and feet tied up. For me, it was a sign from God to better understand what the slave trade was doing to humanity. I understand what you could have gone through, but do you know what brings us even closer?" She blinked and her eyes had filled with more water. "I had twins, and one of them died. Aunty Rose lost her twin, too."

I hugged Mrs Ramseyer tight, and didn't want to let go. What would I do if I found out that Husseina had died? I didn't know where she was, but, in the deepest part of my knowing, felt that she still lived. I would know if she had died. Wouldn't I?

"Talk to Aunty Rose," Mrs Ramseyer said.

It made sense to me now—Aunty Rose's pinched face, her sadness. Aunty Rose taught us English classes and even when there were funny stories, like that talking rabbit in *Alice's Adventures in Wonderland*, she barely cracked a smile. I had never seen her burst into any kind of emotion: not laughter, not passionate cries. Unlike her father, Revd Ramseyer— when *he* was angry, the whole Christian village could hear him railing, and it was usually about the treachery of some heathen chief. And Mrs Ramseyer, the mother of twins—she was anything but sad. But I understood Aunty Rose now.

"Thank you for telling me about your life," I said.

"Let me know any time you want to talk about your sadness," said Mrs Ramseyer. "Do you want me to tell Aunty Rose about this?"

I shook my head no. I had to do it myself. Was it something she talked about with other people? How would I even bring up the subject with Aunty Rose? I plotted. When I wasn't playing with Afua, I spent my time watching Aunty Rose, waiting for the best moment to approach her, but also began to grow fearful of what would become of me if I didn't find Husseina. Sometimes, Aunty Rose would twitch and look over her shoulder, as if an invisible hand had pressed itself there. Most of the time, she held long conversations with the African catechists in the mission, like Brother Stefano, and would break out into belly-holding laughter. I never saw her do that with her parents or the other white missionaries. Other times, she would talk to herself, and I was sure it was to her twin she spoke. In those moments, to make her feel less lonely, I would linger by her.

She led a group of us to the garden next to the big mission house, and I slipped my hand into hers. At first, her hand went floppy, then she looked at me and gripped my hand. We dropped tomato seeds into the holes we'd dug and covered them up with black crumbs of soil. We sprinkled the soil with a light rain of water, then went back to the mission house for lunch. I sat by the other pupils, as we were told to, but I really wanted to take my bowl of boiled green plantain and nkotomire stew to sit by Aunty Rose, who was at table with the other teachers.

During nap hour, I couldn't sleep. I thought and thought about Aunty Rose and her twin and then I thought about their God. Mrs Ramseyer had told us that good things happened to people who followed their God, so how could their God have punished these people who were supposed to be doing his work? They'd left the comfort of their family and the things they were used to, had come all the way to a new land where people looked nothing like them, and yet he had had them imprisoned and had taken away one of

Mrs Ramseyer's babies. I didn't understand why bad things should happen to them. The way I understood it at least, with our Otienu, our God, it could simply be the destiny of the person. Everyone was born with a specific journey. That was it! I would talk to Aunty Rose about her God, and then, if I was feeling bolder, I would ask her about her twin.

I got out of bed and left the dormitory, even though we weren't supposed to go out during nap hour. I ran across the lawn we had freshly mowed that morning, which had left fat blisters on my thumbs, and went up the stairs to knock on Aunty Rose's door.

She answered it and let me into her room, without asking questions. She had no photographs or paintings on her wall, making hers one of the plainest rooms in the mission.

"Why did your God take your twin?" I blurted, out of breath. My mouth acted faster than my brain.

She closed the door behind her and drew up a chair for me to sit on.

She lowered herself on to her bed.

"Mama must have told you then," she said, staring into the air in front of her. "I was a baby when it happened, so I have no memory of it. How much do you know?"

I repeated everything Mrs Ramseyer had told me.

"The people who took my parents prisoner, they made a doll out of clay, painted it white and told them it would help me feel less alone. My parents didn't dare say no to the Asante, but as soon as we left, they destroyed it. Said it was a fetish. I wonder how I would have felt if I had been allowed to keep it." She stopped, sighed. "I honestly don't know why he didn't survive. He was a boy. God has his reasons for everything. Maybe it was to teach my parents humility; maybe it was to save their lives. Maybe when our captors saw that we, too, experienced loss and heartbreak, it endeared us to them."

I saw that I was making her sadder, so I said, "Sorry." I was thinking I really didn't like their God at all.

"I have a twin," I volunteered. "But I don't know where she is."

Aunty Rose stared at me, then quietly said, "You have to find her."

It was not what I'd expected to hear from her, so I said, "She's in a place surrounded by plenty of blue water."

"Tell me more," Aunty Rose said.

"I dream of her a lot. But once in a while, I dream her dreams. That's how I know where she is. I can't control when I get her dreams."

"Hassana, please, whatever you do, find your sister. You have to."

If I knew how to, I would have done that a long time ago, I almost shot back. She asked me to repeat the dreams and everything I remembered. She was beginning to annoy me.

"You're too happy here," she concluded.

"I'm not that happy. I'm quite lonely…"

"You're not unhappy. There's a pattern to everything you've told me. It sounds as if you dream her dreams when you are unhappy. I don't know about your sister and if she has the same experience, but *you* need to feel deep sadness to have that openness to her."

I hadn't realized this, but it was ringing true. Even as little girls, some of the times we'd had dreams in common were when our grandmother didn't want to sing with us because we'd stayed too long at the waterhole, the time our father went missing and when I got into such a sorry state at Wofa Sarpong's. Aunty Rose was probably right.

"How do I get sad?"

"You can't stay here any more. You have to leave. My parents won't let you be sad—they don't believe that children should be unhappy. Yes, sometimes, Revd Ramseyer is like a dragon, but have you noticed how after he shouts he always brings a fruit or something nice to cheer you up? It's too happy here."

"Where will I go?"

"It will make sense for you to go to the coast if you see a lot of water in the dreams. Maybe she's there. And if she isn't, when you know more it will be easy—you can get on a ship and go. You're looking at me as if I'm asking you to do the impossible. Where would you go?" She looked up at the ceiling and pinched her lips inwards. "Not to a Christian family, because Mama and Papa know all the Christians here… Look, I made some friends when the Hausa constabulary came to town. A very nice man called Osman. I'll send him a message and ask if they can host you. In the meantime, you have to do something difficult. Call your sadness to you."

As if Revd and Mrs Ramseyer knew of my plan, they brought me so much good news that I couldn't even will myself to sadness. It was a funny thought, calling on my sadness. Sadness which should have been kept hidden in the shadows, and here I was searching for it like it was a loved one. Mrs Ramseyer told me I had made so much progress with my reading that I could start teaching the younger ones how to read in the small children's school.

I loved teaching so much that I kept thinking of finding songs and tales to share with the little ones. But there was work I didn't enjoy, too. They used our bodies to carry the blocks for building another boarding house.

Time flew by, and I didn't experience my sister's dreams. Aunty Rose would give me accusing stares and I began to avoid her, because it felt as if I were failing her.

I turned twelve, and they moved me out of the room with the other children and gave me my own space in the new building we'd helped put up. Afua cried as if I were abandoning her. Aunty Rose cornered me as I was laying down the sheet to make my bed.

"I told them a long story explaining that to teach you need space to yourself," she said. "Now, do what you can to find your sister."

That night, I thought of the last images I had seen of my mother and of our village burning to the ground. I wound myself into a ball of sadness that didn't lift even as I slept.

Our hair rays out from our heads like large petals. Suddenly braided, her hair grows longer than mine. It becomes a long unending road.

My dreams grew stranger, but they still weren't Husseina's dreams.

I turned thirteen, and Mrs Ramseyer said I would be just the person needed to convince people in places like Asante that they could learn the Bible. I just had to be baptized. I told her I didn't feel ready. Her bright eyes dimmed.

"Hassana," she said, "you'll have to be baptized if you want to continue doing this kind of work. We're letting you teach the very little ones, but if you want to grow, you yourself have to become a Christian. You can't stay a heathen forever."

The word *heathen*, said so innocently, stayed with me. It weighed on me as I considered it with my tongue. It carried with it uncleanness, the opposite of everything good. I knew many heathens, and they were far from unclean and bad. I could lie and say I accepted the new name they would give me, let them pour water over my head, just to keep the peace. But I didn't want to be dishonest. When I shared this with Aunty Rose, she shocked me by saying that finding my twin was more important than being baptized. Towards the end of the year, when Aunty Rose was charged with going to Accra to meet new missionaries who had come down, she said she would take me with her. It led to the biggest fight I'd seen at the mission.

"The girl is staying," boomed Revd Ramseyer. "It costs too much to travel to Accra. We need her to go to Kumasi. The only way the natives will believe is if they see someone like them."

"It would be good for her to come with me," said Aunty Rose.

"Accra is no place for a thirteen-year-old," said Mrs Ramseyer.

"She will be with me," said Aunty Rose.

"She is bright and the mission needs her, and that is settled," said Revd Ramseyer.

They went on and on until Revd Ramseyer bellowed that there was no more discussing the issue.

That night, I was roughed awake by Aunty Rose, who told me to get dressed. The mission was so quiet I could hear her raspy breathing. I got up and my knee bumped into the chair by my desk. Aunty Rose, whose face I couldn't quite see, must have been glaring at me.

"Quick and careful," she said.

I slipped on my frock, and took my atlas and two other dresses the mission had given me. Aunty Rose threw in my Bible, which I was about to leave behind. Then we crept out of my room and down the stairs. In the dark of night, we met two boys, a porter and another, who would chaperone us down to Accra. I was sad I didn't bid goodbye to Afua, who was such a shadow of a person; I hoped she would fare well without me.

Travelling to Accra involved two days of walking, and it was the opposite of the trip I had made to Abetifi, where we had climbed higher and higher. To get to Accra, we descended the mountains.

In Accra, Aunty Rose and I squeezed into a go-cart

meant for one person, with two men pulling us in front and two men pushing from the back. They dropped us at an area close to the sea, and I found myself struggling to breathe because the air was damp. There was a constant slap of water hitting a wall. Once my body adjusted, the air felt less like it was squeezing my lungs than it did in the mountains. Accra was a mad world, especially because I was so tired after our journey. It held more people than I'd seen anywhere else. There were houses that beat the mission house in size and there were many of them.

Aunty Rose said she would take me to Private Osman's home before she went to fetch the missionaries, because it would be easier for her to recount a story that didn't have too many witnesses. She would tell her parents that I ran away, which was not uncommon—I saw six people run away from the mission in my time there. Always, they went to Accra. I wasn't too pleased about Mrs Ramseyer thinking of me as an ungrateful heathen runaway, but my reputation could take a beating. I had to find Husseina.

Aunty Rose spoke to Hajia Shetu, Private Osman's wife, whose husband wasn't at home but had been expecting us. Aunty Rose stuffed coins and notes into my palm. She grabbed me by the shoulders, stared down at me, and urged me to keep believing I would find Husseina. She then pulled Hajia off to the side of the mud-coloured house. I felt naked as I waited for them. When they came back, Hajia asked me how I was in Hausa. I said I was fine. She asked me how I ended up at the mission, and I realized how much language

I had lost when making sentences became difficult. I could now speak Gourmanchéma, Hausa, English and Twi, but the first languages I learnt were being swallowed by the new.

It was almost as if Hajia were just waiting to see Aunty Rose's back disappear for her to reveal her true self to me. Her gold-toothed smile, which I'd found so welcoming and warm, drew into a stiff lip. I wondered if I would end up like one of the heroines in the stories Aunty Rose had introduced me to, a maltreated child.

"You have to earn your keep here," she said. "We're not European missionaries who can just feed mouths. You cook, clean and wash in this house, and even better if you find work."

I wanted to run after Aunty Rose, to tell her there had to be another way to find Husseina, but the way Hajia had filled the doorway with her frame, blocking off the sunlight, I knew it was hopeless. She shoved past me and went to the right of a small corridor, drawing a curtain aside.

"You'll sleep here," she said.

It was spare, but not in the way the rooms at the mission had been. This didn't look like a bedroom—at least there we had raised beds and windows that overlooked gardens and hills. Here, the walls were the colour of mud, the bed was a mattress on the floor, and this was clearly the storeroom for Hajia's numerous basins. There was a small window, but it was closed. I opened it, and the view was the wall of the neighbour's house. I decided to find work as soon as I could, make money, and get out of Hajia's house.

*

This plan was not going to be as easy to do as I thought, because Hajia made sure my days were filled with *her* work. She sold waakye, rice and beans, outside the Supreme Court building, where the people who bought her food were not the court workers, but people who had come to present their cases or those accused of one thing or another. The first month, she wouldn't let me out of her sight. In the mornings, I would clean the bathroom, boil beans, winnow rice, prepare her bowls, make breakfast for her husband and two sons, and then when the boys had left—Private Osman for the Salaga market, and her sons for makaranta, to learn at the madrasa—I would clean all their rooms, bathe, and then accompany Hajia to sell rice. My brain shrank every day I sat there preparing banana leaves for her customers. So whenever I got even a tear of a newspaper, I would sneak it into the basket of leaves so I could read with the early morning light. At night, I didn't have a lantern and candle with which to read.

It was lying there in the dark, one evening, after about two months of the same routine, that my sadness took over me. It lulled me into a deep sleep, one in which my body grew so heavy that it would take a rough shaking to bring me back to waking life.

It's raining. It is lush. My feet are planted in black soil. My neck cranes up and the house I'm standing before is brick orange. Before me are people—women—dressed in white. White scarves, white blouses, colourful necklaces, arms adorned with bracelets. They are about to dance.

I was back in my body, sweating, with a strange sudden impulse to slide my hand between my legs. Down there it was liquid, thick in a way it had never been before. I rubbed its slipperiness between my fingers and brought it close to my nose. Blood. I was bleeding. I had expected that this would come some day, but I didn't know how soon. Although my legs felt wobbly, I kept my fear tight in my chest. I'd seen my elder sister go through this every month. She would take bundles of cotton from Wofa Sarpong's farm and place them between her legs. I didn't have cotton just sitting around, but I had my clothes. I had one nice dress Mrs Ramseyer had sewn for me, the dress I had worn to come to Accra, made of the softest cotton. I was sure I wouldn't be wearing a dress this fancy in Hajia's home. I reached for my sack of clothes and felt around. When my fingers grazed its lightness, I pulled out the dress. I felt for a seam and tugged at the hem till I heard a tear, and then I ripped the dress into strips, swallowing the gulp that had suddenly blocked my throat, because I had no nice dresses any more. I made twelve strips, so I could have four bundles of cotton that I could wash and reuse.

I suppose it meant I was a woman now—Aminah made statements like this to my questions about why she was bleeding—but I didn't feel any different.

When I lay back down, I went over the vivid dream that had brought on my blood. The people were dressed so differently from everyone I'd met on my journey so far. They didn't look like we did up in Botu, with our light cotton clothes. They didn't look like the people of Kintampo in their colourful wrappers, and they didn't look like Mrs Ramseyer and the other missionaries. So far, I hadn't seen anyone dressed in such a way in Accra. People either wore long ground-scraping robes, or wrappers, just like they did in Kintampo. Was that how people dressed where Husseina was?

The month of Ramadan came, and Hajia stopped going to sell her food. I had never felt so hemmed in in my life. At least Wofa Sarpong's farm was filled with trees we could sit under when we finished our chores. Here, the only place I could retreat to was the storeroom I called my room. Her boys weren't going to school either, so the small house shrank in size as we filled up its rooms. Then there was the heat. It was the kind of heat that cloaked one's body and left a film of sweat sticking to one's skin. It was the kind of heat one couldn't escape. Inside or outside, it was the same. But I couldn't stay indoors for so long, so often, in the afternoons when Hajia was asleep, I would sit on the stoop and read the newspaper clippings Private Osman brought home for me. He couldn't read himself, but it was when he brought back a pound of beef or the kola nuts he spent his days chewing that I could get newspapers. I hadn't realized that he'd noticed, but he started taking out whatever it was that had been wrapped in the newspaper, then he quietly handed it to me. There was the *Gold Coast Echo*, the *Western Echo* and *Gold Coast People*.

"What does it say?" Private Osman would come outside and whisper sometimes.

The British and the Asante—that was all he wanted to know about. Two powers that had already fought three wars, and were on the brink of another.

From the newspapers, I knew that the British government, based here in Accra, wanted to go to war, simply to bend the people of Asante to their will and have them included in what they called "the protectorate". Private Osman was like my baba: both were quiet men who were drawn to fiery woman. Because of that, I indulged him, telling him about the Asante delegation's failed visit to England to plead to be left alone. I told him about how the government was asking for recruits from the people under its protection in the Gold Coast to fight the impending war with the Asante, and so far, the Ga chief had refused.

"If you're called, will you go?" I asked him.

"A soldier has to do his duty," he said.

I would support Private Osman and the British, especially because it was the same Asante who had kidnapped the Ramseyers, causing Aunty Rose's twin to die.

When he went back inside, I would read topics that interested *me*: debates taking place in Cape Coast, which seemed to be a far more interesting place than Accra. I devoured articles about the end to the practice of slavery. Then I came across an article from the *Western Echo* called the "Ladies Column". Parts of it were stained with palm oil, but what was legible asked women not to: *endear themselves to being experts in the rules of Domestic Economy... The nineteenth century calls... for a more exalted and grander work; and that work is the cultivation of intellect.* This was just what I needed to hear. Hajia's work was drying up my brain and I could have been teaching, doing helpful work, not washing dirty bowls. Also, I needed more money.

It was the push I needed. I went to Hajia that afternoon, when she woke up from her nap and after she'd said her Asr, the afternoon prayer.

"I have dreamt of my sister," I said.

Her eyes shot up in surprise for a few seconds and she collected her face.

"And?"

"I would like to find other work, so I can make money to find her."

"You're free to work anywhere you like. No one is keeping you here by force. Next thing I know you'll take me to the tribunal for forcing you to work for me against your will... You can go anywhere you like."

From the papers there were stories of people being written up for slave trading and owning, but I had come willingly to Hajia's, even if it was true that I was in a situation no different than when I'd been with Wofa Sarpong. I knew she and Private Osman were keeping me here as a favour to Aunty Rose. There was no way I would accuse her of anything. I just didn't want to do the dull work any more.

"Thank you," I said, opening my eyes widely.

"The rules are still the same. You still do your housework while you're here."

My first big breakthrough came the day Private Osman sent me to pick up his uniform, needed for the military undertaking being called the Second Expedition to Asante. He occasionally sent me on errands near the market— distributing kola nuts to his friends, mostly.

"Go to Scissors House," he said. "It's not far. They have a sign, but if you get lost, ask anyone for Shipemli—it means *inside the ship*."

As he instructed, I walked along Zion Street, up to Horse Road and turned right. And there was the building, painted in green and yellow. I stepped in the first door under its sign, where I met a file of men about Private Osman's age, also picking up their uniforms. I stood in line behind them as they chatted away in Hausa. The ones ahead of me hadn't seen each other since another war in Kumasi twenty years ago. They asked each other about soldiers they'd served with and seemed very glad to have reunited. It filled my heart with excitement. The day Husseina and I saw each other, what would our reaction be?

When it was my turn, I mentioned Private Osman's name and said he couldn't come himself, but showed the man behind the counter what the private had given me as proof of who he was.

"Tá bom," said the man with light brown skin, who searched through a rail of uniforms behind him.

When he gave me the uniform, crisp and black, I thanked him. My eyes travelled above him, to a picture of a seated woman with a white scarf around her head, her neck and wrists piled with necklaces and bracelets. She wore a lacy white blouse. Below her, letters were inscribed, but they were too small for me to read. The hair stood up on my arms.

"Who is that?" I asked him, pointing to the picture.

"Minha mãe."

"What does that mean?"

"My mother."

"Where is she?"

"You certainly ask a lot of questions. This was in Brazil. But she's with the ancestors now."

Finally, my dream had led me to the name of a place. I had more questions, but other soldiers had shuffled in behind me, waiting to pick up their uniforms. I thanked the man and went back to Hajia's house.

I handed Private Osman his uniform and he smiled, patting the uniform's buttons, with an expression I read as pride. I wondered what it would be like to fight a war, but I had more pressing thoughts: I had to locate Brazil. I dashed to find my atlas. I studied the African map, but couldn't find a place called Brazil. When Hajia called me to come and help her in the kitchen, I still had not found Brazil.

I needed to work before night fell, so I took the atlas, sat on the stoop outside and placed my thumb on Accra. I remembered the water. Brazil had to be a place across the sea, so I traced my forefinger over the big blue of the sea and moved downwards, because it seemed the easiest place to go. I went in a straight line and when I hit land there it was, a big land shaped like a chicken thigh. Brazil. That's where my sister was.

I had to find an excuse to go back to see the man in Scissors House, so the next day, I told Hajia that I'd left something there. Luckily, I met the same man sitting behind a machine that reminded me of a horse.

"I want to go to Brazil," I said to him.

"Good morning, little girl," he said. "To do what in Brazil?" he asked, peering over his glasses, a tape measure draped across his shoulders.

"To find my sister."

"It's a big place. She's in Rio de Janeiro or Bahia or Pernambuco?"

I'd only looked at where Brazil was on the map and didn't know these places he was talking about. My head hurt. With every step I took, the gulf between Husseina and me widened. Was she even thinking of me? Did she get into *my* dreams?

"Sir," I said. "What do they call you, please?"

"Nelson."

"Mr Nelson, did your mother dance?"

"She loved to!"

"Do people only wear white in Brazil?"

He laughed deeply. "Many do. Mostly for ceremonies."

"How do I go to Brazil?"

"Ship."

"Is that why this place is called Shipemli?"

"People say we came from a ship. Some even say our building looks like inside a ship."

In the corner of his room sat a mountain of yellowing paper. I thought fast.

"Do you have a bookkeeper?" I asked.

He shook his head.

"I am magnificent with words, numbers and keeping order. You can pay me to keep your books, and I'll let you tell me everything I need to know about Brazil."

The man laughed and held his chest.

"Fine, little girl. Only because you remind me of my daughter."

If Husseina spoke in her dream, I now had someone who could interpret her words for me. Maybe she would say where she was living.

CHAPTER FIVE

Vitória

Salvador da Bahia was like the yellow inside a flower. It was the moment after rainfall, when the sun shone in full force. It was every skin shade in the world gathered in one place. As she and Yaya rumbled along in a steam tram, she marvelled at how rich everything was around her. It was as if she were seeing, smelling and tasting for the first time. In Bahia, like a snake, Husseina moulted, shedding the pain of her name and past, and fully embraced Vitória.

When they had first arrived in Yaya's small orange brick box of a house resting on a hillside, a whole group was waiting for them. Mostly women, they had lined the house's corners with white and red blooms, had cooked beans, roasted a suckling pig, fried plantains, and doused gari—which they called farina—with thick palm oil. They fussed over Vitória, clutching her to their chests and making sure her plate was never empty. She felt a part of them, even though she didn't always understand what they said, especially when they spoke in rapid musical bursts. She loved that Yaya's neighbourhood was called Liberdade. It made her feel as if she were kicking sand in the eyes of the people who had raided her village and kidnapped her. Now she lived in a place called Freedom. She was Vitória and she lived in Freedom.

Yaya had quickly climbed back into her old habits and wasted no time in planning and organizing a Candomblé ceremony, to be held that weekend. Vitória wondered when the novelty of this place would wear off. How different from Lagos Salvador was! Even Yaya was different here. It was clear the Lagos house was her dream house, inspired by some of the large homes Vitória had seen in Salvador. Here, Vitória wasn't sure Yaya could afford a house that big, but in Lagos, she could. Here, Yaya bowed when she had visitors, her shoulders rounded in a posture Vitória read as sadness. In Lagos, people bowed at Yaya's feet. Yaya shrank in Bahia, but there was something here that kept her coming back.

They arrived at the market. Vitória was used to markets being open affairs, but here the sellers had stalls under a big pavilion. Although they sold goods she was used to seeing—meat, fish, vegetables—some leaves and twigs looked different. Yaya went round stocking up on these unfamiliar items. When one woman offered Yaya kola nuts, Yaya shook her head, proudly proclaiming that she'd just come back from the motherland with a fresh load. They went to the animal produce section, which reeked of raw flesh and chicken faeces. Yaya bought three white chickens, which the seller trussed at the feet and put in the basket Vitória was forced to carry. The only comfort she found was that their beaks had also been tied up. They bought so much food that they had to hire two boys to carry their goods back to Yaya's house.

They'd arrived in Bahia just as the rains were starting, but it didn't look as if a dry season was ending. Back in Botu, everything would have been shrivelled and powdered in red dust. In Salvador, plants were still green and flowers blossomed in their pinks, yellows and oranges. As Vitória climbed up the hill, she was surprised to find a colourful garden in front of a house not very different from Yaya's but inscribed on its wall were a moon and star. The etchings were so faint, one could easily have missed it, but she hadn't. It had to be a mosque, which was surprising. It was like seeing a lion bathing in a pond. Out of place. In Lagos, there were churches and mosques alike, but she hadn't seen anything like a mosque in Salvador. Churches stood on every corner. As were terreiros, temples tucked away in homes and in forests—as Yaya's was. She filed away the mosque in her mind and took up the basket of chickens, leaves and gnarled twigs.

The purchases would be used in a ceremony to be held not in Yaya's home, like they did in Lagos, but instead in a small temple lodged in a forest. Vitória, Yaya and some of the women Vitória had met at Yaya's spent the Saturday cleaning the dusty, mouldy temple hall, and putting up palm fronds to keep away bad spirits. Vitória couldn't understand how dry and wet lived together in Salvador. The place was dusty and mouldy all at once. They tied up strips of red cloth on columns and on anything that lent itself to binding. Red. Xango's favourite colour. Xango. The orixá that had chosen Yaya.

In a small room, Yaya and a woman named Maria, who insisted on calling Vitória Bela, did the cooking. "Bela, but why are you so beautiful?" she would say. No one had ever called her that before.

By evening, everyone had changed into long, full-skirted white robes. Three young men arrived early. Two sat behind atabaque drums, long and wooden and crisscrossed with ropes, and one shook a shekere, which came alive with the rattle of a hundred cowries against a gourd. Vitória served them glasses of water and watermelon juice. The one in the middle smiled broadly and her heart twitched. She smiled back. Yaya settled in a large chair that made her look like a queen as the congregants came into the temple.

Even as more people trickled in, Vitória couldn't help but search for the boy's face. This was new to her, letting her heart dream. She joined the women on the left side of the room. The men sat on the right. A gong beat and the drums started, leading some of the congregants to stand up. They sang, clapped and filed around in a circle.

Two people, one a man, the other a woman, whirled in as the drumming intensified. They moved light and fast, their feet barely touching the ground. A young woman moaned loudly and fell to her knees as she received her orixá. Sister Maria and another older woman dashed to her and mopped her brow, moving her closer to the drums. Another man rocked forwards and backwards, sliding into a trance. Many others went into trances as the singing carried on. Yaya escorted the first man who had received Xango into a side room. The congregants continued to sing songs of which Vitória knew only a few, mostly by tune.

The part she loved began. Someone dressed as Xango emerged through the same door Yaya had exited. He was dressed in a crown with red beads veiling his eyes, his neck was ringed with red beads, and he wore a red wrapper around his waist. He held two axes and took wild beautiful sweeps around the room. When the drumming stopped, Vitória's gaze shifted to the drummer in the middle whose face glistened in sweat.

The ceremony ended and Vitória dashed to the kitchen, having completely forgotten she was supposed to be dishing out food for the guests. Sister Maria was there and passed the plates to Vitória without reprimanding her. Vitória served the guests their plates and ambled between the ceremony hall and kitchen. When she arrived in front of the drummer, before she could stop herself she said, "You play beautifully. My name is Vitória."

"Joaquim," he said. His eyes were green, in contrast with his skin colour, which was darker than hers. He started wiping down his drum. "Ah, you're Yaya's god-daughter."

She nodded.

"Before the ceremony, she told us you just came in from the mother country. I would love to visit Africa."

Vitória stole a glance at Yaya, who had her head bent, whispering to another older lady in white and bursting into belly-deep laughter.

"Tell me if you need anything," Joaquim said, wiping the sides of his drum. Then he pointed to the congregants. "These people don't know it, but I'm the mayor of São Salvador."

"Mr Mayor, will you show me *your* Salvador?" she asked.

"With pleasure," said Joaquim.

The wait for their rendezvous felt eternal. Everything in between came disguised as a chore. Like when Yaya made her cook whale meat, which was the strangest meat Vitória had encountered. It was soft, but couldn't decide if it was more like chicken or fish. In any case, she wasn't eating it. It was for an important guest who had a special taste for the stuff.

When the guest came, he was an older man who, in greeting, pinched Vitória's fingers as if they were soiled and sat at the edge of his seat. He and Yaya talked so fast, it was often hard to understand them. It was all talk of politics, and how because of some war going on in the hinterland of Bahia, Yaya had to be careful with the Candomblé ceremonies. Vitória was slowly beginning to understand why, before coming to Bahia, Yaya had told her to profess to be Catholic. Yaya said in the past, enslavers didn't want the people they'd bought practising their own religions, so people pretended to be Catholic and just converted their orixás into Catholic saints. It was not safe to be anything but Catholic. Since Yemanjá had chosen her, she should hold dear the Virgin Mary, Our Lady of the Conception.

The man held everything so delicately, Vitória had the impression that he himself was so light she could blow at him and he would fall over. His skin was almost transparent, and his brows and moustache were thick and white. When they sat at table, he picked around the plate of green plantains, whale meat and vegetables, and it wasn't until he left that Yaya called him a canalha. A scoundrel.

Vitória, on her way to the kitchen with the dirty dishes, had seen Yaya fold something into his palm. Some réis, Vitória was sure. How much, she could only guess.

It was in moments like those that Vitória wondered if life wasn't better for Yaya and herself in Lagos, but Lagos had Baba Kaseko.

Vitória hadn't told Yaya that she and Joaquim had planned an excursion. She didn't know why she already felt guilt when she'd done nothing wrong. She put on a long yellow dress and parted her hair, slathered it with coconut oil, and braided two cornrows that fell on her back.

"You look nice," said Yaya.

"Thank you," said Vitória. She paused, then blurted out, "Joaquim is taking me around."

Yaya puckered her lips, shrugged, and said, "He's a good boy. Well brought up. You see the sun coming down, you're back home."

Three claps blasted in from outside, announcing someone's presence at the door. A beat later, she realized the claps had paralysed her so much that it was Yaya who'd answered the door. She was nervous.

"My son," said Yaya. "Take good care of Vitória, enh? Come back before dark."

Vitória stepped out on to the flower-lined path in front of their house. Joaquim wore a simple white shirt, brown trousers, a straw hat and no shoes. He had clearly not put in any kind of time and effort. But his simplicity had its charm.

He walked backwards and pointed at the houses and said, "This is our quilombo. We've lived here since the first slaves decided to flee here, away from their slave masters. This is why it's called Liberdade."

Vitória knew that in Bahia every single day bore reminders that slavery had been declared over only a few years before. Like the fact that Yaya and the other members of the terreiro couldn't worship openly and still hid behind Catholic saints. She wondered if Joaquim had known servitude like she had. But she didn't like thinking of the past. Instead, she asked him where they were going.

"I'll show you my favourite places."

They walked down the hill, past the mosque-like house, and to the main street, where horses and carts raced by and where trams puffed by along their tracks, with a *chuku-chakachukuchaka* sound accompanying them. The bay lay to their right and they strolled along a mostly abandoned street, until they arrived at a square with a flurry of umbrellas under which women sold fried acarajé in oceans of palm oil. It was almost like Lagos, but the sounds were different. People sang when they spoke. They waved at Joaquim and teased him about Vitória, slapping their thighs as Joaquim wagged his finger at them. Bare-chested men carrying loads in and out of shops stopped to tease Joaquim, too. He was popular.

"These ganhadeiros have nothing else to do but gossip. They have no respect for their mayor."

At the top of the incline, they came to a cobble-stoned square surrounded by yellow, blue, light green and pink buildings. Those buildings always reminded Vitória of the cakes Yaya Silvina baked for Yemanjá ceremonies.

"Pelourinho," he said.

"Who doesn't know Pelourinho?" said Vitória.

"I'll show you another side of it."

A woman perched behind a big basin of bubbling palm oil beckoned them over, and Joaquim waved back.

"She is the only mãe I go to. Tudo bem, Mãe Stella?"

"Tudo bem," said the large woman, who scooped out golden balls of acarajé into a basket next to her.

Joaquim bought them a banana leaf full of the crisp bean cakes and thanked Mãe Stella.

In front of a purple, run-down house, Joaquim pushed in a door streaked brown and white by rain and sun. They landed in a room filled with faded armchairs oozing cotton wool from their upholstery. At the feet of the furniture sprouted weeds. Vitória trod on the weeds and twirled.

"Welcome to my home," she started, but Joaquim sobered her thoughts.

"When slavery was abolished, they ran away."

They. Vitória was sure he meant white people. Pelourinho was the place in which slaves were tied to poles and flogged publicly for disobeying their masters. Vitória shuddered at the thought of what Joaquim or his ancestors, or even Yaya, may have suffered. She was sure the white people fled because they feared for what would happen to them.

He led her up the stairs, past ghostly rooms and on to the balcony. There, they could see the whole square, the rooftops of the church of Rosário dos Pretos and beyond to the bay.

"We live in a beautiful place," she said.

"Beautiful but haunted," he said.

Shouting flared up from downstairs. Vitória didn't have to crane her neck too long, as a group of children appeared, pushing and shoving each other. One boy ran ahead of the pack and stuffed his face with a piece of acarajé, one he was probably meant to share with the others.

"Orphans," Joaquim explained.

"Where do they sleep?" asked Vitória, thinking of how she could have ended up without a roof if Yaya hadn't saved her from Baba Kaseko. Their faces were covered in dirt.

"In these houses," said Joaquim. "And one of my favourite orixás, Ibeji, protects them."

Vitória knew about Ibeji, and had been doing everything to avoid situations with the orixá of twins.

Joaquim asked her if she'd ever attended the Ibeji festival. She shook her head no.

"We'll go to this year's. At the festival, adults have to wait till we've finished eating before they are allowed to eat. I wish every day was Ibeji's day."

Hassana would love such a celebration, Vitória thought, and shooed away thoughts of her sister. Instead, she watched

Joaquim as he talked, noticing freckles on either side of his cheek, and that when his lips cracked into a smile his front tooth bore a small chip. He took her hand and they walked back downstairs and outside. At a fountain covered in blue and white tiles, Joaquim crouched over and let the water spill into his mouth and out along his neck. He wiped his mouth with the back of his hand. Vitória found his gestures simple, with no pretence. He was the complete opposite of the man who had visited Yaya's house. The scoundrel.

"Why isn't it safe to practise Candomblé?" Vitória asked.

"Who said that?"

"It's just a conversation I heard."

"Here there are two kinds of people. For some people, Africa is everything. And for other people, Africa is nothing. Worse than nothing. Our skin, our food, our beautiful Candomblé—they want to take it away from us. They send the police to break us up. They close down our temples."

Vitória was sure Yaya must have been paying for their temple to stay open.

They passed by majestic buildings that appeared so empty that it must have been only ghosts who lived in them. They went to the Elevador Lacerda, which Joaquim proudly proclaimed his pai worked on. It took them from Pelourinho, high on its cliff, to the port below. They walked along the shore, and Joaquim had so much to say that she didn't notice they had gone round in a circle. Before she knew it, they were at the foot of their hill in Liberdade. He led her to Yaya's house and promised to show her more.

*

In Salvador, Vitória's day-to-day was almost a mirror of her life in Lagos. She made clothes with Yaya; she took part in ceremonies. Many times, Yaya mentioned how Vitória would be given more responsibilities in the temple after her initiation, but she had to come of age first. Vitória looked forward to the day when she would be dressed in Yemanjá's beautiful blue and white frock, dancing gracefully during a ceremony.

As for the sewing, here it was particular and far more specialized. Many women came to Yaya for clothes for their ceremonies. The skirts were made with special cotton that had to be cooked in boiling water and starch. It took many attempts for Vitória to learn how to starch a skirt. Then, Yaya started teaching her lace-making. The first lesson, Vitória poked the wooden needles on her thumb so many times she cried. Yaya had said that a real woman knew how to endure pain. Before she could stop herself, Vitória retorted that she was a girl, not a woman.

"Yes," said Yaya. "Real women don't run around with boys."

Yaya's words didn't stop her. Her friendship with Joaquim grew stronger, and they went on many walks. Most of Salvador's corners, inclines and shadows grew etched into Vitória's mind and, soon, she knew it better than she did Lagos—at least Pelourinho, its lower cities and Liberdade. In places like Campo Grande they would be so obviously out of place that she and Joaquim never went there. There, he insisted, even the weather was like in Europe. Their walks were a good time, and they would twist and wind around the city with no goal but to eat, laugh and find strange things to watch. There was always some new surprising detail. Like the church they walked into where Joaquim vigorously crossed his chest and kissed his thumb. Its walls were filled with gold. Vitória was surprised it was still standing. Joaquim told her the gold was from the motherland. Somewhere else, the church would have been raided a long time ago.

Her life's beat grew into a nice tempo: stitch, attend ceremonies, wander around with Joaquim.

A few months before her fourteenth year, after two years of living in Bahia, Yaya told her she had to end her excursions with Joaquim.

"He's a nice boy, but you're a very pretty girl, and now you've got your blood. If your mother were here, she wouldn't let you go with him, would she?"

Vitória's heart hurt. She wanted to point out that Yaya wasn't her mother, but that would have been ungrateful to a woman who *had* become her mother. And if Na had been around... Vitória couldn't even begin to fathom what her mother's reaction would have been. Before Vitória had left Botu, Aminah had been only a year or two older than she was now, and the only time a man came over to express interest, he was as shrivelled as the dried fruits people liked eating here. Na and Aminah had schemed and sent the old man packing. Vitória didn't know how to navigate these matters of the heart, but she was sure her mother would have told her to listen to that beat in her body. Na would definitely not have mentioned Vitória's beauty—she loved saying you can't eat beauty.

"You're not going with him next time," said Yaya, stirring a pot on the stove.

"Why, Yaya?" said Vitória.

"You've had your blood and men… well, young or old, you can't trust them to have control. He's only what—fifteen? If he wants you, his mother should do the right thing. In my day, proper young ladies weren't even supposed to be seen outside." Then she sighed, and said, "I'm making feijoada with the bacon and beans cooked just the way you like."

"I'm not hungry."

"Now that you're a woman you start preparation for your initiation tomorrow. You need strength. That's also why I'm telling you to stay away from *that* boy. You have to focus."

Yaya did everything she could to fill up Vitória's days with initiation preparation. Vitória didn't know if Joaquim came to look for her, because they spent days buying fabric and other sundries Vitória would need for her time in seclusion. It made Vitória dislike the idea of being a novice, but she went through the motions, every day growing a button of anger in her chest that came out in little puffs, uncontrolled, usually when Yaya asked her to run an errand or to prepare something to eat.

The big explosion occurred the night before she went away for the initiation. After days of not seeing Joaquim, she was climbing up the hill when she espied him and a group of Liberdade boys gathered around a berimbau player. She loved the sound of the berimbau, with its distinct bow-like shape and ball and string. One lithe boy jumped to his feet and started flipping his body. She waved at Joaquim, but he took so long to respond that she put her hand down and was about to continue climbing up, when he got up and came to her. He wouldn't look her in the eye, and kept staring off in the direction of the sea.

"It's been a long time," Vitória said.

"Yes."

"How are you?" It wasn't the question she wanted to ask him. If she'd been braver, she'd have said, *"Did you come to look for me?"*

"You should be stronger," he said. "Know what you want and then fight for it." Then he went back to his circle of friends.

She couldn't believe he'd just left her as he had.

When she got home, Yaya, holding a piece of cloth, rattled off a list of things Vitória still needed to do: find an old dress, find a blade; she needed this, she needed that...

"I'm tired," said Vitória.

"That's the way you talk to me now? Ay, Xango, how people change. Don't forget who you were when I took you in." Yaya clutched the fabric to her chest then went to her room at the end of the corridor.

The words cut. Vitória hadn't expected Yaya's reaction. She hadn't expected to be reminded of the past. It made her feel as if she'd been stained and even several washings wouldn't take the stamp of *slave* away from her. She felt dirty inside and out and wanted to be scrubbed clean. It was as if Yaya were saying, "*How dare you dream? How dare you try to love?*" As if she didn't deserve any goodness. Only pain. Or was it because she was trying to forget? Was Yaya telling her that forgetting the past was a bad decision, because it would only come back to haunt her? The day she was split from her family, she decided she would never look back. She chose to live; she chose to create a new life. Was that decision turning its neck back around to bite her? If Yaya was telling her not to forget, it was forgetting that had saved her. Madness would have been her path had she not forgotten.

She went to bed with such sorrow filling her heart that she didn't think sleep would come, but it did.

The roar of waves lashing against the shore is deafening. She shades her eyes and considers the wideness of sea. A rough sea. Less calm than the bay. The water is grey and the sky is cloud-filled. Heavy. Are you there?

The next day, knocks woke her up from her terrible night. She barely had time to think through her dream, because Yaya had pushed in the door and was sitting on the bed. She wrapped her arms around Vitória and massaged her shoulders.

"I just wanted to make sure you learn all the rites quickly. And what I said was unkind—it was the last thing I should have said to you. I know what it's like to belong to a person. We're the same."

Vitória decided she would do the Candomblé initiation and become a very good student to please Yaya. As for Joaquim, she would have to encourage him somehow. They would have to do a slow dance, but it was the best way. She didn't want to lose his friendship.

Vitória and three other initiates were carted deep into a forest behind Liberdade, where they were secluded for a month. The forest had an opening carpeted in thick vines, and an altar covered with Catholic saints and sculptures of different orixás, such as Exu in a top hat and Yemanjá in her blue dress with pots of water. The initiates lived in huts that reminded her of Botu, but the huts were more solid and colourful in Botu, whereas here they were made of mud and twigs.

The initiates first went through a haircutting ritual. When the razor touched Vitória's scalp, she cried. Seeing her hair fall in clumps around her feet reminded her that this was another new step in her life. She had never cut her hair, and now it was all gone. Then the barber made a nick on her scalp. She knew this would happen, as a way for her orixá to make her entry, but it still frightened her.

Yaya came and went and taught them songs and dances. One of her first lessons was: see, don't speak. There were things that didn't need to be explained.

In front of the altar was where, after throwing sixteen cowrie shells against the dust of the ground and singing, the babalorixá said Yemanjá chose her as her daughter. He cast again and said he was also getting messages from Ibeji. He strung together clear beads and ringed Vitória's neck with them. Every day she had to learn both Yemanjá and Ibeji's songs and dances and the foods that made both deities happy. Yemanjá's were mostly white: rice, corn, white kola nuts and onions. Ibeji liked sweets and rice and chicken and a thick okra sauce, caruru.

The isolation she felt and her closeness to Ibeji made her think of Hassana more than she'd wanted to. She missed her sister, but was thriving without her. And besides, it was Hassana and others in Botu who had stunted her growth. How many voices had she heard growing up that told her she would never amount to anything without her sister? It was those voices that choked off her tears when she rounded the bend with the human caravan and saw the last of her sister. They thought Vitória weak, a half-formed thing, who needed to suck off her sister's strength to survive. She'd wanted to prove them wrong. So she fought every connection with Hassana that was threatening to come in.

And yet, every day, she had to fling open doors to her past to let Ibeji or Yemanjá use her as a vessel, and it was a struggle, not only because she'd wanted those doors to remain shut, but also because there seemed to be a competition for the Gods within her, a contest that ended with no winner. In Lagos it had been easy to receive Yemanjá, but that had changed. And maybe the pact she'd made with herself—to make it on her own—was what was holding her back.

Her co-initiates would be taken over by their orixás—one was Xango and the other was Oxum—and it was beautiful to watch the moments when their orixás decided they were ready. One girl, even more timid than Vitória, would transform when Xango entered her body. Her stooped shoulders squared out and her eyes shone wide and confident. She would leap and bound with the warlike beats that accompanied her, not stopping until the drums quieted down.

The babalorixá said Ibeji was a tricky, playful orixá, and could block off Yemanjá just for fun, but Vitória was sure that in trying to forget her past, she was cutting off her sister and that was not the kind of environment Ibeji, the deity of twins, or Yemanjá, the protector of twins, would want to come into.

After two weeks with Vitória still not receiving Ibeji or Yemanjá, the babalorixá cast cowrie shells and said, "You are keeping something from me. One who lies to the oracle is lying to himself."

Vitória said nothing.

"Vitória, you need to be honest with yourself for this to work. The initiation is to spend time with the best and worst parts of ourselves. To acknowledge all that we are made of. You are hiding something."

He looked deep into Vitória, as if searching her eyes would reveal the truth.

She almost told him about Hassana, because she was scared that he would find out himself, but she was also worried about being sent back to look for Hassana. She wasn't ready, so she continued to keep that part of herself sealed.

The man sighed.

"Whatever you're keeping from me, Ibeji is not happy. Yemanjá will protect you no matter what. Don't tell me if

109

you don't want to, but ask Ibeji for forgiveness, and they might show you the way."

She had done nothing wrong. Their rift was not her fault, she thought, but the babalorixá gave her such a piercing look, one that she was sure would crack her open and pour out her secret, so she muttered desperate prayers to Ibeji.

"You are the ones who open doors on earth; you are the ones who open doors in heaven. When you awaken, you provide money, you provide children, you provide long life. You who are dual spirits," Vitória recited.

The story went that Xango and Oxum had the first twins born on earth. Seen as an abomination, Oxum was kicked out of the village. She abandoned her twins and lost everything, including her sanity. Yemanjá took the twins and protected them. If worshipped well, they would bring great wealth—otherwise, they could also bring misfortune.

Knowing what she knew of Ibeji, she left sugar cane for them at the entrance to the hut she slept in, and told them she was sorry she hadn't been honest to the babalorixá. She wanted to be a good follower and would do whatever it took.

Every time Ibeji's drums were played, Vitória would dance and dance and feel no different, not even experiencing the tingling in her toes she sometimes felt with other orixás. She was ready to give up, to tell the babalorixá, to maybe try a different orixá who would accept her, but was so scared of the babalorixá finding her out that she kept away from him.

The babalorixá said there wasn't an initiate he hadn't been able to make receptive. He told Vitória to pray that Yemanjá would receive her during the outdooring ceremony, during which each initiate would come out of seclusion and would receive their orixá before a big audience.

The day of the outdooring, the initiates were covered in white chalk. Vitória felt nervous, for good reason. The forest grove filled with people from Yaya's terreiro, as well as many new faces. The babalorixá came around, drawing circles and etching lines in their skin. She saw Joaquim and her heart raced. She didn't know he was going to drum during their outdooring. No one said anything to them, as was the custom, and they had to sit down and face down until their music called them.

Libation was poured. The babalorixá started singing, and the gathered went round dancing and clapping. The Xango initiate was the first to go and the bellicose drumbeats warmed up everyone. The next was Oxum's and the dance flowed fluid and feminine, and the initiate, although a boy, was the most beautiful person in the whole forest. When Yemanjá's drums began, Vitória got to her feet and placed her arms on her waist, wing-like. She shuffled forwards and backwards and the song began to speak to her.

She floats. Around her is a beautiful sweet song that lulls her. She becomes water, buoyed by a force that feels like home, like waves, like a mother's embrace. It is in her and about her. She is shrouded by home and love and she is brave.

Vitória came to, and Yaya wiped her face. Her skin was covered by a wash of sweat. She felt so relieved that Yemanjá hadn't abandoned her, that Ibeji hadn't punished her. Beyond the relief was also a sense of awe. She couldn't believe she was one of Yemanjá's now.

After the ceremony, everyone hugged the initiates and a big feast was unveiled. There was so much to eat, and Vitória wolfed down the corn and palm oil, cooked just for her. She hadn't realized the multitude of people who would be present for the initiation. After she'd eaten, she looked about. Some guests sat on mats, drinking from calabashes. Near the altar were the plush seats reserved for the babalorixá and other elders, now empty, and next to them, two drummers cleaned their drums. People in small groups shared conversations and laughter.

"You danced with grace," said a voice, startling her.

Joaquim regarded her with his green-eyed smile.

Vitória fought back tears. "Yemanjá saved me."

"You are one of the few people in this terreiro to receive Yemanjá. Well done."

Now that she'd become one of Yemanjá's children, Vitória found herself looking forward to the ceremonies at the temple.

The third rainy season Vitória had lived in Bahia, a day when Yaya was stricken with her rainy season sickness, the slimy canalha showed up at their door, as he did every six months or so. Vitória showed him to the sitting room and offered him a seat.

"A drink of mango or guava?" Vitória asked.

"I'm in a hurry, so make this known to Yaya. Tell her Senhor Ferreira is here to see her."

Vitória found Yaya propped up against pillows, pushing a needle through a thick weave of fabric. The curtains had been thrown open and a spray of sunshine streamed into the room. Vitória relayed the man's haste to Yaya.

The old lady winced, pushed back her covers, and threw her legs on the floor. She lifted her hips off her bed and shuffled to her dressing table. She tried to shield Vitória from seeing, but Vitória had already seen the money she crinkled into her hands.

"Please change my sheets," said Yaya. "It must smell like sickness in here."

Vitória was sure the old woman didn't want her to see the exchange of money. Just how much was she paying that man and who was he? If it took so much money to keep open the terreiro, why didn't Yaya just stay in Lagos?

Later that day, Vitória and Joaquim walked to the market to buy goods for Candomblé worship that weekend. Every time Yaya was unable to leave her bed, Vitória stole the chance to meet Joaquim. She was shocked to see the slimy man coming out of another house. Who else was he extorting money from?

"That man," said Vitória. "I think Yaya is paying him to keep our terreiro open."

Joaquim muttered something under his breath and spat. His jaw flexed then he said, "They don't want us to be happy."

"I don't know for certain, but he's come by at least two times. And I can't think of why else she'd be paying him."

"Let's talk to Baba Sule," said Joaquim. "He knows everything. Or how to respond to everything. He's not in the Candomblé belief, but he's wise."

They didn't go far down the hill and stopped before the house stamped with the moon and stars. The mosque, finally. She wondered what this friend would be like. The name Baba Sule made her feel a kinship with him already.

Joaquim clapped thrice and a man with a small white beard and a shock of hair beneath his nose answered. On his head he had on a woven cap that contoured his head, just like Baba used to wear, and his gown was like a gown from Botu.

"Baba Sule," said Joaquim. "Good afternoon."

"Welcome," he said.

"Thank you."

Sule pulled back the door to let them in.

"How is our new Yemanjá initiate?" And then, explaining, said, "Your community is kind. Yaya always invites me to witness the welcoming of new initiates, which I enjoy watching. Your ceremony was beautiful. Please have a seat." He pointed to raffia mats on the floor.

The smokiness of incense tickled Vitória's nose. Sule passed to her a bowl of kola nuts and Vitória picked the smallest she could find and crunched into its bitterness. Joaquim chewed it like it was sugar cane.

"How can I help you?"

"I think Yaya is paying someone to keep our temple open," said Vitória. "And I'm confused."

"Policemen came to stop our worship once," said Joaquim. "Yaya spent days going back and forth to the police. We thought it was over."

Vitória watched Sule. His eyes were grey and calm.

"If she's paying him and your ceremonies are still going on, there's nothing to worry about," he said.

"It just angers me," said Joaquim.

"If she didn't do what she was doing, there'd be no temple," said Sule.

He turned to Vitória and said, "Joaquim tells me you're from Lagos. Are you Oyo or Egba or...?"

"No. I'm Gurma." Vitória knew it was a distance from Lagos, but she didn't know how the two places fit into each other, if they did at all.

"I wish I spoke Gourmanchéma. Welcome, daughter," said the man, switching to Hausa.

"Thank you," Vitória said, shocked that he could speak a language she hadn't heard since leaving Lagos.

"To tell you the truth, you didn't even have to tell me. Your face reminds me of home. I would have said you were a Grunshi girl. Do you like it in Bahia?"

"I do."

"Listen, my young friends, Yaya is just doing what she has to do to keep the community together. You'll grow up to find out what absurd sacrifices adulthood forces you to make."

Vitória found herself in front of the mosque a few days later. Maybe because Sule spoke Hausa and even knew Gourmanchéma words, she felt he was closer to home than anyone else—even more than Yaya.

He welcomed her, offering her kola nuts and greetings in Hausa.

"What brings you here today?"

Vitória paused, and then let it all out. "I have a twin and have told no one."

"Do you know where she is?"

Vitória shook her head. Why had she come? This was painful.

He continued, "Back home, if someone lost a twin, we held ceremonies to send off the twin safely, and to keep the living one on the earth. I'm sure your twin is alive, or you would have followed her. You wouldn't be here talking to me. Or you would be very sick."

It was a chilling thought, and Vitória didn't know if she believed him.

"Have you had any of her dreams?"

How did he know? She relaxed a bit and told him her dreams. The most recent was a dream about a building. It was green and yellow. Hassana opened the door and then shut it.

"Twins are one part of a whole. You two need to find each other. It's the only way you two will be complete. You're like half a person without her." Then he added, soothing her, "And she's half a person without you."

She'd felt the opposite. With her sister she'd felt like half a person, but here in Bahia people almost worshipped her—because she was pure Africa, they said. In Botu, people had called Hassana the beautiful twin. "*You look exactly the same, but she's the beautiful one*," they would say. It was bittersweet, this looking to the past. It was easier to look forward, to just start from the part where she met Yaya in Lagos.

"What if I don't want to be found?" she said.

"Ah," said Sule. "I thought twins were bound with an invisible thread."

"I have my reasons."

He watched her, his white moustache still, his eyes not blinking. Vitória didn't like the way he compelled her to fill in his silences.

"I was so small next to her," said Vitória, patting the air next to her as if it were a dog. "And everybody made me feel that way. She had the bigger voice, she was the one they would ask to do anything, and she would ask me to come along only then. There was no space for me to be myself. It was always Hassana and her twin. She caused our separation, but when that happened, I could finally breathe. Be myself."

"Now that you've grown into a strong, free woman, you can surely stand up to her."

"What if she's become worse? She was like that when we were ten. At age fifteen, she could be unbearable. I don't want her to find me."

"That's harsh. You must miss something about her."

Vitória was quiet and stared at the Arabic inscriptions on the wall. She missed the way Hassana had no time for authority and made fun of the village chief, and the way that, without having to say a word, they would burst into laughter. She missed their shared dreams. She mentioned the part about the dreams to Sule.

"Keep listening. She may be looking out for you is what your dream tells me. I'm tired today. Next time you come, I can read the cowries."

Vitória thanked him and walked back to Yaya's house, her eyes glued to the ground. She worried about what the cowries would reveal. What if her sister was terribly ill? What if she had to return to Botu?

Baba Sule called her back a few days later and said he had time to do her reading.

When he threw his cowries, he said, "She is far away, there is sea separating you, but she is closer than she's ever been to you. The two of you make one. Like a circle, this is a journey others have gone on before you. You were sent to learn, and you now have to complete the circle. It's taken you from here to there, and now you have to come back to each other."

"Please explain," Vitória begged.

"The djinns, that's all they have for you. You will have to make sense of it yourself."

She wanted to scratch at her insides, itching with impatience and annoyance at these mysterious messages. She would have liked a message that simply said Hassana was alive and well, not one that was forcing her to go back. She didn't want to leave Salvador.

CHAPTER SIX

Hassana

The first day of working with Mr Nelson, I made sure before I left that the house was immaculate—Hajia wouldn't even be able to find one cockroach leg.

I had just walked out of the door when Hajia stuck her head outside and said, almost like an afterthought, "You're still eating your meals with us." She barely smiled and went back inside without waiting for my response, but her words warmed my heart, because I would still get to eat meals that reminded me of my na's cooking. Hajia felt like family, and her prickliness made me think of Issa-Na, my baba's second wife. And because of that, I didn't dwell on Hajia's manners towards me. I was also convinced she was lonely, since Private Osman had left for the Asante expedition a few days before. The British had put together a large force of soldiers like Private Osman to march into Kumasi, the Asante capital. When his company—about ten men dressed in sharp uniforms—had come to pick up Private Osman, Hajia, her boys and I stood outside, waving farewell. The man was beaming, and I felt proud that I knew him.

I walked into Scissors House, and Mr Nelson, bubbly with a dimpled smile, herded me into another room through a side door, his sitting room. There, he had gathered all the papers that I'd seen and more. The papers were as high as me.

"You asked for employment. Here you go. These are orders, receipts, bills, maybe even letters. How do you plan to start?"

"First, I'll categorize them, arranging them by date, then create a log of everything. I'll need something to write with, a ledger, a ruler and folders."

"You *are* good," said Mr Nelson. "I have the writing material. As for the folders, I'll buy them for you later."

I was grateful I'd paid attention in Abetifi. At the Basel Mission, everything had its place, and Revd and Mrs Ramseyer would sometimes ask me to fetch clearly labelled dossiers. They could account for everything: every single person who had visited them, every shilling they had spent, every piece of wood that went into their buildings. I took a look at the pile before me, and my palms sweated and my eyelid began to twitch at the amount of work I'd have to do, but it was better than selling food. Right then, my nerves turned to pride. I was glad that I would earn money I could give to Hajia, money I could use to buy newspapers, money I could save up to buy a ticket for a ship to Husseina. I could already taste the ink of the ticket, clasped between my lips as I stood on the ship's deck and looked out on the shore I was leaving behind.

My work lasted four hours every day, with a short break in between. It was during one such break time that I went into the courtyard of Mr Nelson's house and my gaze fell on the brightest, most mischievous set of eyes I had ever seen. She closed her eyes, sucked deeply out of the white stick in her mouth, threw it on the floor and crushed it underfoot.

"Don't tell my father," she said in English. It was perfect English, with no trace of a Portuguese accent. "Augustinha Amerley Nelson. Just call me Amerley."

I took her outstretched hand and shook it.

"Hassana."

"I hope my pai is paying you well. He tried to get me to do that drudgery, but I have no patience for that kind of work."

"He is precious," I said.

"What are you doing this afternoon?" said Amerley. "My grand-uncle, Mr Brimah, hosts horse races every Thursday and Friday. I have a horse I think will be lucky today. Join me?"

After working, I usually went back home to Hajia, had lunch with her, washed the dishes and read snippets of the paper or, if I had nothing to read, I would wander around the zongo, the part of town where mostly people from the north lived, just before the dark set in. I'd never been to a horse race, and it sounded like a chance to break out of the everydayness of my life.

"Be here at three in the afternoon," she said and went up the stairs into a room that must have overlooked the sea.

I ate Hajia's tuo and ayoyo soup with relish and went to my room to dig in the box that housed my clothes. I didn't have one presentable item of clothing. Everything was worn or yellowed. I decided on a simple white dress with buttons on the front. I slid it on and it was so tight it flattened my chest and belly, but there was nothing else that I could wear.

Hajia was beached on the mat in the sitting room, while her older son sat copying Arabic letters from a prayer book into a notebook.

"Hajia," I said.

"Yes?" She didn't lift her head.

"I will be late for the evening meal today."

She seemed to mull over what I was telling her, her jaw ground. She finally said, "They say if a vulture pleases you, you will miss the guinea fowl. It's the man you work for? He'll keep you from finding your sister."

I couldn't help but laugh. I hadn't realized how invested Hajia was in my work of finding Husseina.

"Oh, it's not a man. Only Mr Nelson's daughter."

"Ah," Hajia said. "Then go and come. Don't forget truth lasts longer than a lie."

Hajia's proverbs reminded me of my grandmother's. Women like them were moulded to not trust anyone, not even themselves.

When I arrived back at Mr Nelson's, he was in the cutting room in the front of the house, talking to a customer. He waved at me without asking questions, so he must have known I was meeting Amerley. I walked through the courtyard and up the stairs, and for a second the sea drew me to her expanse and I wondered which direction along her eternal horizon would lead me to my sister. Then I continued up the stairs and knocked on the door that I'd seen Amerley open earlier.

"We need to get dressed," she said, pulling me into the room.

I tried to press out the creases that seemed to have multiplied in my dress.

"We go as men. Luckily, my father gives me the clothes I ask for. You are so small," Amerley said, peeling off the clothes she was wearing and dumping them on top of the other clothes that had made the floor their home.

The room had a fragrance that reminded me of flowers, but I didn't have a name for them. I wanted my mind to be filled with the knowledge of everything—flowers, clouds, smells, inventions, politics—and it made my chest itch that I didn't know so much about the world.

Amerley pulled open the door of a solid mahogany wardrobe and extracted two pairs of green riding trousers. She gave me a white shirt and she herself chose an off-white linen shirt. For the first time I felt self-conscious about my body, and turned to face the window that overlooked the sea as I pulled off the dress I was thankful to be rid of. I wondered if my body was pleasing to look at, if it was beautiful. My sister Aminah was a girl that everyone desired. She didn't like that. Was it better to be desired or left alone? I felt Amerley's gaze on my back as I put on the shirt.

"We should get you a corset," said Amerley. "They keep breasts perky."

I'd read about corsets in the Ladies Column, but they'd seemed so removed from my world.

"Will your father make them?"

"Oh no. No, no. Too complicated. Next time, we'll go shopping in Christiansborg. I would give you one, but mine are so worn… and my dear mother used to say you can share anything you like but not intimates."

I turned around and she was naked from the waist up. In front of her chest were breasts that reminded me of the baobab pods that held the sweetest fruit. She would need a corset, of course. My breasts were like garlic buds on my chest.

"Where's your mother?" I asked.

"She passed when I was six. She was sick. But old Mr Nelson has done good work raising me by himself, wouldn't you say?"

She threw on her shirt and went to a brown box on her desk. She popped open its lock and flipped through it, her fingers like little dancers.

"Stunning, wasn't she?" she said, pulling out a photograph and handing it to me.

Her mother's hair fell in ringlets around a delicate face. What I would give to have a picture of my mother and sisters.

Her mother looked light-skinned. Amerley's skin was slightly darker than mine, reminding me of Husseina. I wondered if, with time, we'd come to wear the same colour skin, or if she would bake browner. My skin seemed to be growing lighter the older I grew.

"Were you born here?"

"Right here in this house. Can you believe my parents first met on the ship coming from Brazil? She disembarked in Lagos, and he came to Accra with his family. It wasn't until my mother visited an aunt, years later, that she found my father again. She had difficulty having children, then one day I was here to stay. And that is my story."

Amerley didn't ask me any questions, so I didn't volunteer my story. Instead, I tucked my shirt into my trousers like I'd seen her do. I was not talking also because Amerley was revealing some interesting information: there was a ship that must have gone from Brazil to Lagos to Accra. What if Husseina had done the reverse and ended up in Brazil that way? Would retracing my sister's steps lead me closer?

"Have you been to Brazil?" I asked.

"Never."

"But you call yourself Brazilian?"

"That's what my father says we are, but honestly, I feel more Ga than anything else. My Portuguese is deplorable."

She threw a beaver hat at me.

Thinking of all Amerley had told me blurred my vision during the short walk to the polo grounds and throughout the races, which were entertaining but not an activity I planned to spend many an afternoon on. Amerley went every week. She won money at the races. She lost money at the races. She tried to make me bet on her horse, but money was not something I planned to play with. That day, Amerley's horse, a grey dappled creature, lost.

Amerley smoked a pipe and looked out at the dust settling on the racecourse.

"I should start doing the opposite of my desires," she said, the twinkle in her eye betraying no sadness.

Soon, Amerley was always waiting for me during my pause. She would give me newspaper clippings she found amusing or offer a fruit from one of her aunt's gardens. Sometimes, after work, she walked home with me, a chance for her to smoke her cigarettes. She was a welcome break from the monotony of arranging papers and keeping Mr Nelson's books; after a while, bills and receipts all began to look the same.

Two months went by like that, until one evening, after returning to Hajia's house, we found Private Osman sitting on his stoop. He'd been away since December of the year before, 1895, around the same time he'd asked me to go and retrieve his uniform from Mr Nelson. I felt grateful to him for this errand because it had not only taken me a step closer to Husseina, but it had also gained me a new friend in Amerley.

"Evening, sir," Amerley and I chorused.

His eyes went up and his lips moved, but made no sound.

"Tomorrow, Hassana," Amerley said, waving at me.

Private Osman was wearing the same uniform I'd picked up, except what had once appeared sharp and pristine was now frayed at the sleeve, covered in dust, its trousers replaced with blue and white batakari trousers. He rested his chin on his spread-open palms, staring into the air. I sat by him. What had happened to that smile he'd left with? He didn't look at me, but acknowledged my presence with a sigh.

It seemed like a whole hour had gone by before he said, "They make war sound glorious. 'We're putting an end to the slave trade,' they said. 'We are ending human sacrifice. This will make the Gold Coast safe.' But was it worth the lives lost? I got so sick in Cape Coast it's only by Allah's will that I recovered and could come back. They've sent the Asante king to Freetown, but the Asante are a force. Between here and Freetown, whether it's by sea or by road, they will find a way to stay strong. Too much sickness and death. *Kai!* War is no good. The old Ga chief, he was right to say no to helping the British. He was the only wise one in all of this. And then they don't pay us well. *Kai!* War..."

I sat there with him for most of the evening, as he repeated the refrain "War is no good". Even as I fell asleep, I heard him shouting, "*Kai!*"

We are selling food to the caravans, singing our song, "Massakokodanono". People pass by; others weave together fronds for their tents; some buy our millet cakes. A fire breaks out and spreads fast. I hold her hand, but she grabs it back. I throw sand into the fire, now close to us. It does no good. She stands there, dancing.

The next time Amerley and I met, after that strange evening with Private Osman, we left Scissors House and, with the sea to our backs, went back up Horse Road and wound into our zongo. Even though she was brash and seemed worldly, I got the sense that she didn't leave her home ground much, or at least her world of Brazilians. In the market, butchers chatted loudly and hacked at chunks of meat. They waved at me and I waved back, filled with pride that they saw me as one of their own. This was *my* chance to boast.

We walked by women selling waakye, men trading in fabric, and ended up across from Mama Z's Pito Parlour. I'd dreamt many times of sharing this with Husseina, who would have enjoyed laughing at the patrons of this place. Husseina, quiet and shy as she was, was drawn to less respectable moments of life, like when we saw four feet in a caravan tent, or when we eavesdropped on the gossip the Botu wives whispered about their husbands. I was happy I could do this with Amerley. We shared a large stone as a seat and watched Mama Z's. We laughed till our bellies ached as people staggered out, yelling curses one minute and clutching their hearts and dancing the next minute. Whatever pito contained, it turned grown men into comedies.

At Hajia's house, we weren't laughing, however. Private Osman grew stranger and stranger. Whenever I returned, whether in the morning or in the evening, he would be sitting on the stoop, lamenting the bad nature of war. At night, he yelled till his throat was hoarse, and his children, then eight and ten, came to my room to get away from their father's terrified rants. It softened Hajia, rounded her edges, and she began to look to me to help with her boys.

I was happy walking them around the zongo and picking them up from Koranic school after work. It made Hajia so warm to me that when I asked if I could spend the weekend at Amerley's, she didn't even send me off with her usual admonishment. I needed just one night of sleep in which I didn't hear throaty screaming.

On that afternoon, after work, I took my raffia basket packed with my sleeping cloth, a change of clothes for the next day and a dress that Amerley had given me and went across the courtyard to Amerley's room. She wasn't back from her classes, so I set my basket down, opened up the windows to air out the room's stuffiness, and looked at the books on her shelf. I picked up one, *Jane Eyre*, that lay on Amerley's bed and started reading it.

I woke up to Amerley's big smile hovering above me. She was her father's daughter.

"I am so giddy you're staying over." She'd thrown her schoolbooks on to the floor and flung herself on the bed. "Today, we go to High Street to get that corset. Tomorrow, we'll go to my cousin's wedding, and then on Sunday, church."

For my part, I felt like I'd gained a sister, and my happiness was so large it blocked out any words, so I just ended up grinning like a fool.

"That book is dull," Amerley said. "See, it lulled you to sleep."

"I was enjoying it! I have just been sleeping badly where I stay." It hit me that I didn't have a home. I couldn't use the word *home*—hadn't had one in a long time. I was floating.

As if she'd read my mind, she said, "Why do you never tell me about yourself?"

"You never ask."

"I shouldn't have to. I blurt out every unimportant detail to you."

When I was at Wofa Sarpong's, my voice left me, and I didn't think it had come back yet. And now, Amerley took up all the space, didn't let me feel like my story was important, so I didn't try to make my voice heard. It made me think of Husseina and how she rarely spoke. If anyone asked questions, I would answer for her, as if she had no voice. For the first time, I understood what she must have felt like.

"Where is your family from?" Amerley asked.

I sat up, fluffed up her pillow in my lap. I told her about growing up in Botu, a place which was beginning to feel more and more unreal since I hadn't seen it on a single map; I told her about our village getting burned by slave raiders, about losing my twin sister, about hopping from place to place.

"And now, here I am."

Amerley's eyes were welling up. She shoved me on my shoulder.

"You should have told me this a long time ago. How do we find your sister?"

"I dream about her all the time. Sometimes, I even have her dreams, but it's been so long that I'm not even sure if she's still alive," I said, voicing a fear I hadn't wanted to acknowledge. "Even those dreams now seem like childish longing. Maybe my mind gave me dreams that tricked

131

me into thinking they were hers. Hajia always says that to make the heart eat is to bring on hunger. The more you want something, the more you think about it. Honestly, Amerley, I think I'm losing faith."

"NO!" Amerley bellowed, taking me aback.

"I think she's in Brazil," I said.

Amerley got up and put her hands on her hips. "My father and I haven't kept links with Brazil, but I'm sure one of my aunts knows people who go back. Hassana, don't give up. We can think of a plan as we're shopping."

To get to the trading post, we wove through roads that bent and curved, split and fused together without end, and eventually reached High Street, facing Ussher Fort, a building built by the Dutch and now being used as a prison. The papers constantly mentioned overcrowding in there. I'd passed by High Street a few times with Hajia in the days when I sold food with her, but had never ventured beyond it to Christiansborg. Amerley and I continued on, loitering by small shops peddling pots, basins and cloth, until we arrived at a part of the street that suddenly seemed greener, like another country.

"Where's this?" I asked.

"Victoriaborg."

The houses were different from ours in the zongo, on an even grander scale than Amerley's house, painted white from roof to foundation, with large gardens surrounding them. Some buildings even stood at three or four storeys. Even the way the trees shot up from the ground seemed to say that this is where the rich live.

"Do African people live here?" I asked.

"Not many. My father's doctor. Some lawyers. Only *very* sophisticated blacks from Sierra Leone."

"The air smells nicer here. Something is missing."

We kept walking, and then it hit me.

"I can't smell the lagoon. I can't smell smoked fish. It's unfair. We live in the part close to the lagoon and the Europeans get to choose dry land?"

Amerley shrugged.

I'd also read in the papers that there were land disputes between the European government and the local kings, and I didn't understand it all, but I felt as if we were always getting a bad deal with the Europeans. Private Osman had gone and fought their war and come back, luckily with his body whole, but his mind and spirit broken.

We walked some more, by the greenest grass, some of it well trimmed, other parts looking treacherously long, and in the distance there was what seemed to be a small lake. We stopped in front of a huge building with two storeys which reminded me of the mission in Abetifi. When I saw that it *was* the Basel Mission Trading Company, I froze. What if Mrs Ramseyer or her husband were there? I didn't want to appear timid to Amerley, so I swallowed my fear and followed her.

The store was guarded by a man in an unironed uniform. I went in and a thousand different fragrances fought for attention—some enticing, like the smell of new, others off-putting, like the smell of sweaty feet. Above us hung rows of bicycles, and I wondered how they'd been suspended.

Amerley didn't linger the way I wanted to. To her, this was old news. She cut through aisles lined with shelves holding sugar, cans, bottles, fruits and biscuits of the sort Mrs Ramseyer and her family served during special occasions. We passed by a beautiful pyramid of lamps, cane chairs and sturdy-looking desks, then stopped at a section with only clothes, folded on shelves.

When I saw the price for a small dress, my eyes bulged. Three pounds. I couldn't believe anyone had that kind of money to spend on a dress. I made one pound a month from working with Mr Nelson and paid Hajia fifty shillings, half of my salary, for my keep. I wouldn't be able to afford the corset and I didn't want Amerley to spend that amount of money on me. She was sifting through dresses and placing them against her body, and I started doing the same to distract myself from the heavy breathing coming out of my mouth. Who could buy these things?

Amerley dragged me over to the shelf with corsets, piled on top of each other, and there, too, everything was pricey. She picked a corset, a black and white one with black lace trimming, didn't look at the tag, and said we could go and try it on. In the changing room in the back, a young woman looked us over and, maybe on recognizing Amerley, let us pass. I was sure that if I'd come by myself she'd have turned me away. Even the guard at the entrance wouldn't have let me get this far.

I had to disrobe in front of Amerley, who I was beginning to get used to. She really did feel like a sister. To put on the corset, I had to suck in my belly and hold it for seconds while Amerley helped me hoist it up. Once it was up, I tried to let out my breath, but it was stuck, right under my throat.

"I can't breathe," I said.

"Good, it's working."

"I really can't. Get it off!"

"That's how corsets work."

"GET IT OFF!"

Only then did she relent.

I was so happy I'd found it uncomfortable.

"In any case, my breasts are small," I said.

"You lucky thing," she said, pinching my breast. "Here is an idea. You should write a letter to a Brazilian newspaper about your sister."

"In what Brazilian city? As your pai pointed out, it's a big place."

We left without spending a shilling, and I was relieved.

I hadn't slept in the same bed with anyone since I left Aminah in Wofa Sarpong's farm—even in the Basel Mission we slept on our own cots—and it was comforting to have another body by me, never mind that it was a body that snored. As the snores kept me semi-awake, I listened to the sound of waves crashing. They cradled me to sleep, then, minutes later, Amerley's snoring would wake me up. One would think I would have considered it a bad night, but I dozed happily.

"Pull," said Amerley, the next day, with her corset around her hips.

I tugged hard and up, and she fell down on the bed. I laughed, but she was not joking. We tried again and again. We were supposed to be at the church by ten, but by the time we got Amerley into her corset and then a floral dress with bell sleeves, it was well past ten. I slid on a yellow dress she had given me. She combed my hair up, pulled it into a bun and slid a butterfly pin into the bun to keep it together. Amerley did her own hair. Truth is, apart from two cornrows, I didn't know how to do hair. Aminah had always done my hair.

I was expecting the wedding to be over and done with by the time we arrived at the church, but to my surprise, only the groom and the guests were there. Amerley must have had foresight. The church, luckily only a street away from Scissors House, was a brick edifice that was more ornate than the mission church. Inside, it bore sculptures of Yesu splayed on the cross with a crown of thorns, a scene I knew well from all the Bible study we'd done at the mission even though my imagination was so different from the reality I was shown here, because in the mission they'd mostly used words to describe him, not many images. Candles were lit on the altar, and the people who came in crossed themselves before sitting down.

The church was hot. The sleeves under my arms were stained with perspiration and I wondered how Amerley was able to breathe with the corset squeezing her innards and with all that she was wearing. The organ played a tune that sounded more dirge than wedding song as the bride walked up the aisle with her father, and we stood up, while I wondered how she, too, was able to breathe. She was veiled from head to toe in white silk, and wore a white long-sleeved dress with, I was sure, a corset underneath it all. The men, too, were roasting. Most wore black jackets over white starched shirts and constantly mopped their wet brows. The people who looked the happiest were the men who had thrown their traditional cloths over their bare shoulders and shorts. How I wished I were one of them. The service was the longest I had ever attended. We had to stand and sit so many times, I was tempted to just stay standing.

"If I had to choose," I whispered to Amerley, "I'd rather be Protestant than Catholic. This service is long and boring."

Amerley winked, then caught herself, crossed her heart, and shushed me.

By the time the priest announced that the couple were man and wife, half of the congregation was asleep.

The wedding only became interesting in the subsequent ceremony. We met in a big house in James Town—built, Amerley said, by a man called Mama Nassu. He was the first chief of the Brazilians in Accra, and this was where they held family meetings. It was now home to Mr Lutterodt. The courtyard of the house was bursting with people milling about: some women dressed in kente; others in white; men in top hats and suits; others in their colourful wrappers. Stools and benches had been placed around basins of drinks. Amerley's aunts were drinking non-stop out of calabashes of palm wine. Amerley and I stuck to nmedaa, a corn drink without alcohol.

One of the said aunts beckoned us over.

"And who is this one with no meat?" Amerley told me she'd asked.

They went back and forth in Ga, then the aunt regarded me, her eyes darting up and down, studying me as if I were for sale. It reminded me of the day Wofa Sarpong picked Aminah and me. My jaw ground, and I must have frowned or made a face, because suddenly she clucked and turned away. Amerley said her aunt wanted to know where I had come from.

"She's a nosy drunk," Amerley said. "Ignore her."

We sat down and ate a bowl of kenkey with fried fish and ground tomatoes and pepper. After living in Accra for two years, I still didn't like kenkey, but the fish was fresh and crisp.

Amerley, licking her lips, suddenly gasped.

"Don't look," she said, shifting her body, so we were now facing the big building in the compound instead of its entrance. "Mr Lutterodt and his son."

Mr Lutterodt was an important lawyer who thought his son and Amerley should be married. His son was nineteen, and we were only fifteen. Mr Nelson wanted Amerley to finish school first, but didn't want to lose Amerley's prospects of marrying up the Gold Coast society ladder, so he'd formed a loose arrangement, tying the two young people to each other. When Amerley was ready, there would be a formal engagement. The only problem was that Amerley couldn't even stand the son's company for short stretches. I found myself secretly happy I could make decisions about my life without my family interfering. I could do whatever I wanted and the thought was dizzying.

We wound around the compound, trying other bites that had been spread out, and I got so full that my belly pushed out and I was again thankful I wasn't wearing a horrible corset. I started playing a game, counting how many of the women had one on, judging by the look of pain on their faces. I couldn't rope Amerley into my game because she was one of them and would probably not have appreciated my humour. In any case, her family members kept asking her about her studies and why she didn't go visiting any more. And then we bumped right into John Lutterodt Jr. It wasn't lost on me how life liked to play jokes. I was trying to find a person, and the universe was doing everything to keep her out of my orbit. Avoiding a person? It was the opposite.

John Jr's skin was coloured light like shea butter even though Amerley told me his white ancestor was from at least four generations ago. He smiled at Amerley and stretched out his hand to shake hers and then mine.

"Your friend is?" he asked.

"Hassana, John."

"Pleasure," said John. Then he just stood there and stared at us. Amerley was right—what a dull person.

"How did you find the wedding?" I found myself asking because the silence was too deafening.

"It was beautiful. When it's our turn, it'll be even better."

Amerley feigned a smile and said she saw her Aunty Adukoi calling her and tugged at my arm, pulling us away.

"Where's your aunty?" I asked.

"I lied. Imagine being married to *that* for eternity," she said, when we had approached a group of women who were even drunker now. In the zongo, and even growing up in Botu, it was unusual to see women drinking. I liked that here they could do whatever they liked. "We can't even have a conversation without me feeling queasy. Let's dance."

Drummers pounced on their drums, playing kpanlogo music, and the aunties shimmied their waists and backsides and lowered themselves to the floor. Amerley and I joined them. I couldn't remember the last time I'd danced. When I was eight or nine? We danced, ate, drank nmedaa, and then ended up in a group of aunties in the middle of telling stories. I told Amerley to translate the funny parts from Ga, but I wasn't really listening. They were talking about the ways in which they seduced their husbands. One said juju; another said it was at the dance in their village. I sat and looked at the sky, deep purple with wisps of clouds surrounding a round moon. Both happy and empty, I wondered how the two emotions could mingle so easily inside me. I was content with where I was, but there was still a vacuum within me. I needed direction, a reason for being here. And yet, at that moment, I didn't want to be anywhere else.

We stayed up so late that church the next day was not even discussed, and I was pleased. I couldn't imagine having to attend another Catholic service. When I said so to Amerley, who lay on her back, she turned to me and said, "So what are you?"

I knew the Bible inside and out, but I couldn't say I was a Christian. And as for Otienu and my old beliefs, I felt as if I left them behind in Botu. I *was* floating.

"I don't know," I said.

"You should get baptized. At least that way your soul won't end up in hell."

"When I lived in the mission house, I asked one of my teachers about hell. I said that sometimes this life has felt like hell. Seeing my home burn into flames, with my mother in there somewhere... it doesn't get worse than that. She had nothing to say to me. As for what I remember about our old way of believing, our God grew angry with us only if we'd done something wrong and then we performed sacrifices to pacify him. I still don't know what our entire village could have done wrong to deserve the raiders who came to destroy us. The truth is, I don't know what to believe any more."

"We're still young," she said. "We have all our lives to decide."

Staying with Amerley replenished me and I was able to endure another week of Private Osman's nightmares, but, sleep deprived and scared for what he would do next, Hajia felt backed into a corner. She told Private Osman's superior about his condition, and the man had him institutionalized.

Private Osman had been put away for close to two months, when Hajia, her sons and I made for High Street, walking the same way I'd gone with Amerley, but with a different kind of purpose. While Amerley and I had had time to observe the buildings and people going and coming, Hajia and I walked with dread in our chests. We arrived at what used to be the old high court of Victoriaborg and were welcomed with the words *Lunatic Asylum* etched under the building's eaves. The long entrance was dark and smelt like it had been sprayed with a solution of astringent and urine. At the end of the hallway, a man in white looked up.

Tears had welled in Hajia's eyes and she could barely speak, so I provided him with Private Osman's full name.

"Third floor," he said.

On the first floor, the screams pouring out of the closed doors hurried us up the stairs. The second floor was less noisy; the third floor was quiet as a graveyard. It was also brighter than downstairs. We opened the door to the ward and a row of beds lined either side of the room. I read the names tagged on the foot of the beds, because everyone was wrapped in their own worlds—they were unrecognizable.

When she saw him, Hajia sobbed loud sobs, and a warden told us not to make so much noise. Hajia hugged him and the children went close to their father but wouldn't touch him. He looked at me and nodded. Already a small man, he seemed to have shrunk, and his skin looked wicked of moisture, elephant skin. Hajia opened her bag and took out a green bundle, which she peeled open to reveal kafa, white and tasteless cornmeal, the meal for sickness. Private Osman chewed slowly and looked at his children and smiled.

I wanted to ask someone, anyone, when he could come home, but the wardens—two of them—looked so menacing that instead I turned to Hajia.

"Should I talk to them?" I asked her and she nodded.

I got up, lifted my chin and approached the men. I wanted to mimic the British accent, but I was out of practice from what I'd picked up from Richard, so I simply gathered up my courage and said, "Good morning."

They didn't respond, but at least they were considering me.

"My aunt and I want to know if my uncle is free to go," I said.

"Only the doctor will release him," said one of the wardens.

"Where is the doctor?"

"Go and come. Next week."

Out of nowhere heat formed in my belly and I wanted to shout that they could try harder to care about us. It was unfair and unjust, but I didn't want to do anything that would affect the decision they made. I looked at the other patients and wondered how long they'd been here. They looked rudderless, lost, as if they were just begging to be released from life. That wasn't Private Osman. His doctor had told Hajia that he was being treated for melancholia. He was broken, but didn't want to leave this world.

When I told Hajia, she simply put more kafa in Private Osman's hands, hugged him, and shuffled us out of the hospital.

It was one thing to not know where your family was, but another to see your family being treated badly and being powerless to stop it. It boiled my blood. I knew a person who would take up my case with me: Amerley. We would fight for Private Osman.

"Let's write a petition," she said when I'd told her about our visit.

She tore a sheet from one of her notebooks, set a wooden ruler against the sheet and tore off the rough edge. We sat on her bed with an inkpot and a dip pen, which she grabbed together with a dictionary from her desk. We wrote, scratched out, edited, redacted, until we came up with a neat presentation. My favourite line was: *It is unconscionable that a man who has served Queen and country, in the Gold Coast Constabulary, who, after suffering a mild breakdown, is now being held hostage in the deplorable lunatic asylum. We demand that he be released immediately.*

"What do we do with it?" I asked.

"We'll take it to my father's lawyer friend. He's quite militant."

I was sure the fire I saw in Amerley's eyes matched what I felt in my chest. What if we could became a true force for bringing justice to people in Accra, then spread out to the rest of the Gold Coast? Make people like Wofa Sarpong pay for keeping slaves, hunt down the people who burnt down my village and separated me from my family? What if I became a lawyer myself?

Lawyer Easterman was busy, but asked us to leave our letter in his office. A nagging suspicion told me the letter would end up covered in cobwebs in his office, and with that any dreams I had of defending the defenceless. I wondered what it was that would make me more powerful. Being born into a big Gold Coast family? Being a boy? Not having been a slave?

Amerley clapped and beamed, and we thanked Lawyer Easterman's secretary, but her good mood didn't rub off on me. I wasn't even sure if Lawyer Easterman would read our letter. I didn't feel victorious. I felt powerless.

CHAPTER SEVEN

Vitória

The sky blackened. Thunder rumbled and trees outside swayed as if drunk on pinga. Although it was Vitória's fifth rainy season in Bahia, she could never stop marvelling at how the ground seemed so thirsty—it didn't want the skies to stop emptying.

Yaya hadn't left her bed in a week, and when Vitória entered the old lady's room, she heard quiet snoring. She went to the kitchen and ladled out beans into a bowl and spooned into it palm oil and heaps of farina. She had eaten so much farina and beans, she was convinced she would sprout bean and cassava shoots on her head. Vitória took her bowl into the sitting room, sat at the window, and watched the sheet of rain. Yaya's aches usually lasted a few days. This year, it was troubling how long she'd stayed in bed.

Vitória spent most of the rainy day sewing clothes for their clients, and when the first ray of sun pushed through the clouds, she grabbed a basket and headed for the market. Chicken or pork would break the monotony of beans. When Yaya's bones felt better, at least the house would be in order, the shopping would be done, the clothes would be ready to hand over.

The squawk of a tucano stopped Vitória as she descended the hill. It sounded like a big frog. She looked up and saw the large black and yellow bird land on the top of a cashew tree. Every time she saw a toucan, she couldn't help but think of the tchiluomo, which was what Hassana called their bird cousins, because they always flew in twos. One would call and the other would follow. The ones in Botu were often black and white, sometimes with a red bill, and blessed with a sweet song, far from this one's frog cry. Also, this one looked lonely. She whistled its ugly song and continued to the market.

She came back to the house, left her basket in the kitchen and once again went to see Yaya, who looked shrivelled and grey. When Vitória shuffled closer, she found Yaya's brow dotted with sweat. She brought over a jug of water and a towel and mopped the old lady's brow and her chest. She undid Yaya's tight grey cornrows, slipped her fingers into their coils, and massaged Yaya's scalp. Then she made a tomato soup with pork and took a bowl to her. Yaya sipped slowly, but refused to eat the meat.

Those other rainy seasons, when Yaya had stayed in bed, it had appeared almost like a game to Vitória; it was Yaya's chance to have some quiet before other people came to make demands of her—for clothes, for advice, for guidance, for the ceremonies. This time, it was different. Vitória felt as if she'd been given all her dreams and was about to have them snatched away. She couldn't take care of Yaya alone. She went to fetch Sister Maria, who helped with the Candomblé ceremonies, and came back to Yaya's dark room with her. Sister Maria huffed into the room, and wailed.

"Yaya, you know we all need you here, so please hold on. Fight for us."

When the woman calmed down, Vitória asked, "What's wrong with her?"

"Bela, she's burning hot. A fever."

Yaya murmured.

Sister Maria leant in, nodded, and said, "Vitória, let me look in Yaya's leaves. The medicines."

Vitória went into the kitchen, rummaged in the cupboard where Yaya kept leaves for ceremonies, and returned with a pot of herbs. Sister Maria took a bark and soaked it in a glass of water, then fed it to Yaya's lips. The old lady winced and swallowed the medicine. Then she closed her eyes. Sister Maria and Vitória left the room.

The next days were no better. Sister Maria took over Candomblé ceremonies in the temple, and Vitória prepared food for the ceremonies, shielding Yaya from too many visits. If Yaya had ever said a bad word about a member who came, Vitória wouldn't let them past the door. "Yaya is sleeping," she would say.

Three weeks went by and Yaya refused to see a doctor. She said since she had the orixás working for her, there was no need to see people whose medicine didn't even work. She instructed Vitória and Sister Maria on the herbs they could concoct to make her better. Yaya had lost the tiny bit of flesh that had once given her curves and looked wizened in her bed. Finally, she asked that the babalorixá who had initiated Vitória come to treat her. He stayed in her room the whole day.

Once, unsolicited, Sister Maria let on that Yaya's life had been nothing but difficult. She worked as a wet nurse for a well-to-do family in Salvador, who ended up selling Yaya's children to other plantations. She put away money, coin by coin, until she was able to buy her freedom. It took over thirty years. After that, Yaya resolved to do everything she could to free others. People resisted her because they thought she was buying the people to enslave them.

"Yes," Sister Maria said, "we black people also made slaves of other black people right here in Bahia."

All Yaya wanted was to give them liberty. It was with some of these freed men and women that she started her terreiro, quite late in life, but through that gained many more children than the ones she had lost. Vitória asked why Yaya had come back to Brazil, and Sister Maria said Yaya had told her that the spirits had asked her to do this work of helping everyone break free. Until every one around her was physically and spiritually free, she couldn't stop her work. Slavery was over, but the spirits of people were still bonded.

Vitória stole out in some of those moments that Sister Maria came over, just so she could breathe. She didn't want to feel that she, too, was going to join the ancestors. Often she told Sister Maria she was going to the market, which she did, accompanied by Joaquim. He proposed that they go to Itaparica, the island on which his father had grown up.

"How?"

"I will take you on a jangada."

"I'm scared of water."

"Ah, Vitória! You're a child of Yemanjá."

"You know that sometimes she likes to keep her children close."

"If Yemanjá chose you, she will protect you."

He'd said it with such confidence she didn't quite believe him, but she was ready to trust. It made her think of Yaya's words, that men weren't to be trusted. Thank goodness Joaquim was not yet a man, she told herself and agreed to go with him.

They walked in the opposite direction of town and Vitória turned back to make sure Sister Maria hadn't had her followed. She didn't like the questions the woman asked her when she got back from the market. Why did it take so long? Was the skinny acarajé seller on the road? She was sure the woman was creating some story in her head about where Vitória had been.

At the shore, Joaquim pushed the raft-like jangada in the water with its white sails, the muscles of his skinny arms stretching taut. She marvelled that he walked everywhere barefoot. Growing up as the daughter of a shoemaker, she'd always had shoes—until those horsemen had kidnapped her.

He called Vitória over, but her feet wouldn't lift off the sand.

"Come," he insisted.

"I can't."

"Fine. Close your eyes."

She pressed her eyelids together. Suddenly, she felt herself become as light as air as he lifted her up and put her on a seat in the raft. She opened her eyes. He rowed and soon they were surrounded by clear water. She looked down and saw that the seabed was not far below. Schools of fish darted out of the way of the oars and when Joaquim rowed, the silt whirled up, clouding the clear bay water.

"I could teach you to swim," said Joaquim, releasing the oars and letting the sails take over.

"My sister tried. It won't work."

She faced forward, her neck stiff, and watched the green island of Itaparica grow closer. She quickly glanced at the water, and regretted it. She could no longer see the floor of the bay.

"The view of Salvador takes your breath away from here," said Joaquim.

She tried to turn around but the jangada swayed to the left, so she straightened herself and decided she would see it on the way back. She saw boats loaded with bananas and pineapples heading towards Salvador. A man in another jangada waved at Joaquim. By the time they had rowed through many arms of the mangroves and landed on a sandy beach in Itaparica, her neck was sore. They had been sailing for what felt like hours. The verdant island welcomed them with pastel yellow, blue and pink houses.

"How do we save Yaya's terreiro?" Vitória asked as they walked towards a stone-walled church. It wasn't fair how these churches could be so open, and the terreiro couldn't, just because of where it had come from. "I'm afraid Yaya is dying."

She sucked in a gulp to fight back her tears, and he held her and rubbed her back.

"Yaya shouldn't be the only one putting money into a place that saves all of us," said Joaquim, leading her back towards the sea.

They sat on a small crescent of a beach and watched the endless scuttling of crabs. One crab would go into a hole, come out, discard its load and continue over and over again.

"What if we went around, asking everyone to donate a few réis a month?" asked Vitória. "I don't think we'll get a lot, but it'll be something we can continue giving to that Senhor Ferreira."

"Yes," said Joaquim. "My pai used to say that public figures are such bandits that they'll take anything."

"We'll do this for Yaya—continue the work she started of liberating people and their spirits."

They stared at each other and Joaquim leant in. Their skin touched. He was cool against her warm. His smell was lemony with a touch of salt. Salty? She hadn't realized she'd flicked her tongue against the smoothness of his skin. Before she knew it, his lips brushed hers and she pressed back, and it was the most beautiful experience her body had ever felt. It raced her heart, quickened her blood, and pushed her body against his. He pulled back and looked her in the eyes, and only then did she come back to earth.

He showed her the island's main square, its fort, and made her listen to the delicate croaks of its frogs, in song even in daylight. They walked along the shore, and Vitória was surprised to find that the sea had receded in the short time they'd been there. They would have to take over twenty steps to reach the sea. They stopped in front of Joaquim's father's home and Vitória's heart sank. Green shrubs had overtaken what was left of the red brick. She didn't want this to happen to their terreiro.

When she got back home, Sister Maria's eyes were flooded with tears.

"I think it's the end," she whispered.

Vitória felt guilty for having spent the day with Joaquim instead of Yaya. She felt even worse because she had disobeyed Yaya and continued her excursions with him.

She crept into Yaya's room and sat on the bed, and its creaking woke up Yaya. The old woman's face was smooth, and made her think of her mother's baby when she was born. How could birth and death look so similar? She supposed they were just two extremes of a rope. And a rope could form a circle. What was life but a circle?

"Vitória, go and find her," whispered Yaya.

"Who?"

"Your twin."

Vitória jerked her head back. It took her by such surprise that she said, too loudly, "How did you know?"

"I first suspected you were special when the babalorixá told me you could receive both Yemanjá and Ibeji. But, to be honest, Sule told me. Maybe a year ago or two, he came to find you because he had a reading for you. He let slip that it was about your twin. I pretended to be aware of it. I would never have brought you here if I'd known you were a twin. In fact, I had planned to take you back myself, but this sickness stopped me. Why did you not tell me?"

Yaya pursed her lips and Vitória was quiet. All this time she thought she'd managed to keep this part of herself shelved away from Yaya.

"I didn't... I don't know how to find her," Vitória whispered, sheepish.

"You have to try," Yaya said again, pressing the pads of her fingers into Vitória's wrist.

"I can't just go back to Botu and find her. She was kidnapped, the same as me."

"If she's searching for you, and you for her, you'll find each other. You just have to be on the same land. This water, the sea, it can break connection. It makes things unclear. Cross it and go back to her. You have the same sacred soul." Yaya paused. "I know what it's like to lose family. It can make you lonely and bitter. Find her."

This was not news to her, but it shook up all her plans. Her mother used the word *misuama* for *blood*, and she had often said Vitória and Hassana contained the same misuama. It was why their dreams were connected. But she had other questions.

"Yaya, why was I brought all the way here if I just have to go back to where I started?" Vitória asked. She thought about her work of saving the terreiro, of a possible future with Joaquim.

"Your path will become clearer with time. You're not

the same person I found in the streets of Lagos five years ago. Who came first into the world? You?"

"She did."

"This is important..."

Vitória didn't like the finality of the conversation. It was as if Yaya were dispensing with the last bits of wisdom before she left the earth, and it made Vitória ache. She wanted to leave the room, but Yaya's fingers firmly grasped hers.

"You are Kehinde," rasped Yaya. "It means you came afterwards, but you are the elder. You sent your Taiwo out first to taste the world, and she said it was all right to come out. It means you give the orders. You are the one who holds the key to finding each other. You've always thought yourself smaller, but *you* are in command. Without you she has no purpose. You say the word and she follows. You're the keeper of your joint soul."

Yaya was saying too much. What were these new names, Kehinde and Taiwo? As much as she wanted to have these words translated, she also didn't like the way Yaya's breathing had grown wheezy. She took Yaya's hands in her own and looked into the woman's small eyes. Yaya stared at the ceiling, and Vitória followed the gaze. There was nothing there, but Yaya wouldn't stop looking up. The old lady's eyes grew smaller and soon her breath slowed.

Vitória closed Yaya's eyes. She'd never had to do this for anyone and yet it felt natural to do that, to draw the shades on the windows to Yaya's soul. Then she went out of the room and called Sister Maria, who had been preparing a meal in the kitchen.

"She's left us," said Vitória, heaving into sobs.

Sister Maria began moaning and then humming a song to Xango, Yaya's orixá.

Vitória went to her room and curled up on her bed.

People would come and Vitória would have to go out and greet them—Yaya's funeral was bound to be an affair that would bring people up from as far away as Rio, Sister Maria said.

It was true. The funeral was so large that it was held in one of the bigger terreiros in Bahia. Everyone wore white, and they sang from morning to evening. There were so many people. Too many people. Vitória sat in a corner of the room. Just sat. She hadn't been able to do anything. She'd abandoned her plans to go around canvassing for money. Sister Maria and the other senior members of Yaya's terreiro let her be. Vitória felt as if she'd been deboned. Joaquim brought her a plate of feijoada, which she didn't touch. She'd thought that after everything that had happened with her family, tragedy would leave her alone for a long time, but it was still searching for her. She cried herself to sleep.

She is underwater, breathing. She circles around her sister. She breaks the surface of water, into air, and her lungs expand. She's swimming by herself.

After the funeral, Vitória moved into Sister Maria's home, over the hill from Yaya's. One evening, Vitória heard Sister Maria arguing with her husband. At first, she thought it was none of her business and was going to stay in her room, but when she understood it was because the city of Salvador was planning to close down their terreiro, she went out.

Sister Maria wasn't arguing. Tears snaked down her cheeks; her eyes were bloodshot. Her husband was seated. His bulging eyes regarded her but he said nothing. His skin was drained of colour; he did nothing but drink beer and play board games with his friends.

"They are closing the terreiro?" Vitória asked.

Sister Maria explained that Yaya's good relationship with a politician was the only reason she'd been allowed to practise Candomblé and keep the terreiro open for so long. The city wanted to clamp down on people practising Candomblé so they took advantage of the slightest transgressions. Yaya's only transgression was dying and leaving a congregation motherless. Sister Maria said Yaya had taken her to meet the politician just before she was bedridden and the man had seen them, but when Sister Maria tried to meet him on her own, with money Yaya had left, he claimed he didn't know her.

Vitória remembered the crabs on the beach the day she and Joaquim had visited Itaparica. They never stopped moving. Even when Vitória chased them away, they would stall, and come right back to work.

"We'll go back," Vitória said. Fear was pushing into her belly, but also filling her with a bubble of excitement. "We'll sit outside his door every day. We have the money."

In the terreiro, Vitória had experienced only good things: it was a congregation of people who came together to commune with their ancestors and the spirits that protected them. It was a place where everybody would leave with a belly full. It was a place where blessings abounded. Every time she'd felt Yemanjá in her, she was left powerful, kinder, plump with life. She didn't understand why anyone would want that to end. It wasn't a group of people wishing death on anyone. They weren't condemning anyone's soul to the hottest depths. Everyone was welcome, and Vitória had seen many people come to Yaya's terreiro.

Vitória and Sister Maria went into one of the massive buildings she thought was inhabited by ghosts, because no one seemed to go into or come out of them. She was surprised to find the world it held inside: a sea of white men. These men laughed, slapped each other's backs, and had no time to consider two black women, one of whom was a child.

They asked for the man's whereabouts and were sent down a long hallway to a room stuffed with paper. Vitória was both surprised and pleased to find that the politician was the scoundrel she'd once fed whale meat. She had a feeling that his colleagues didn't know about the visits to Yaya. If he tried to use the same tricks again, she would mention all the times he'd come to visit.

"I'm Yaya's daughter," Vitória said. "From Liberdade."

Senhor Ferreira grinned apologies and excused himself from the men with whom he shared the office, and shooed Sister Maria and Vitória out.

"It's too late," he whispered in the hallway.

"Nothing is too late," said Vitória.

"We have the money," said Sister Maria, patting Vitória's hands to make her calm down.

"And we'll continue to have money for you," bluffed Vitória. "How often do you want to be paid?"

He said nothing.

"We'll keep coming."

"Keep your voice down," said the man. "I'm not making promises, but come back next week and I'll have news for you."

He looked about and raised his brows, his lips and fingers dripping in expectation.

Sister Maria snapped open her purse and took out a roll of réis.

Senhor Ferreira tossed them around for weeks, during which Vitória had a lot of time to think. Yaya's last words often came back to her. And she'd been dreaming a lot about her sister. Mostly dreams of water. She knew she couldn't stay with Sister Maria forever, but the thought of going to search for Hassana made fear grip the insides of her belly with its sharp nails. And then Joaquim. What if they could run off into the insides of Bahia? She could start her own terreiro and sew clothes. Hassana seeped into her mind again. The world was gigantic. The chances of finding her were small. Why should she go through more heartache instead of moving on?

She sought answers. Baba Sule was wisdom itself. She asked Sister Maria if she could go and see him and the woman walked Vitória down the hill and clapped in front of

Sule's door to announce their presence. When he answered, Sister Maria told him to accompany Vitória back home after they were finished.

"Go back," said Sule. "Your bond will be stronger there."

"Yaya said the same thing."

Yaya's adopted daughter, Tereza, was in Lagos—she could go back and stay with her, but Vitória confessed that she didn't know how to write.

"You have a British passport," said Sule. "You'll have no problems going back. Maria and I will write to Tereza. If you ever want to come back, you can. It's only a river between here and there."

If Yaya had been a mother hen to Vitória, Sister Maria was a lioness. Joaquim wasn't allowed to visit, because decent girls stayed indoors and especially didn't receive male guests. Vitória was chaperoned everywhere.

Sister Maria wouldn't let Vitória go to Senhor Ferreira on her own, which Vitória would have gladly done. She would have sat outside his office door from morning to evening to get word from him. Instead, she spent her days finishing up sewing orders Yaya hadn't completed. She collected pitanga fruit that had fallen in Sister Maria's garden and put them in baskets. She waited for her return date to Lagos. This soon grew repetitive.

Vitória went to Sister Maria in the kitchen.

"We should tell everyone that the terreiro will open again," she said, "or they'll move to another temple."

"It's a lot of people, Bela."

"I'll do it. And I'll get the other young ones to help me."

"I don't know…"

"We can't wait for that horrible man. And the more people we have behind us, the more power we have." Vitória wouldn't repeat Yaya's mistakes. If they arrived in a pack at the man's office, he'd be so embarrassed he'd have to act faster. She and Sister Maria weren't enough.

"We'll have to start in Liberdade," said Sister Maria. "Word will spread after that."

"I can begin in Liberdade tomorrow," said Vitória.

"Tomorrow I have many errands, Bela. And I have to be there with you."

Vitória felt precious, and that was not a feeling she liked very much. She wanted to go around without Sister Maria. She stared her down.

"Maybe we can go together in the morning… Ah," said Sister Maria, changing the subject. "We've written to Tereza. When we hear back, we'll buy your ship fare to Lagos."

Vitória would rather have gone around with Joaquim, but the next day, she and Sister Maria went down the hill, past Sule's house and walked up a narrow red path towards the lee end of the hill. They clapped outside the house on the top of the hill and the old man who answered said he wasn't interested.

The next house was Joaquim's, and Vitória sucked in her breath. Since Yaya's funeral, she'd only caught glimpses of him.

"I'm coming with you," he said to Sister Maria.

"You are popular," she said. "And you know everyone, so I can't refuse. We're telling people the terreiro is still open."

"And we're taking contributions to keep it open," Vitória said.

The trio walked silently. Vitória mulled over the many unsaid things between herself and Joaquim. She imagined a conversation between them.

"*We haven't spoken about what happened at Itaparica,*" he would say.

"*There's no point—I'm leaving. I'm going back to Lagos.*"

"*Don't go. Stay here with me.*"

Arriving at the next house drew Vitória from her thoughts. There, the woman who answered said she had moved on, to a different terreiro. In another home, an older woman flapped her arms in the air and said Yaya would be proud of them. Down the hill, they picked up cousins of Joaquim and Sister Maria, all young people who wanted to help in whatever way they could. Vitória stole the chance to sidle up to Joaquim.

"I'm going back to Lagos," she said.

He was quiet, then said, "I admire that you're still working for the terreiro. You really are a wonderful person."

"Thank you." She was grateful he didn't get upset.

They swelled in number, and at one point, they had to stop and tell people why they had congregated. Sister Maria and Joaquim both turned to Vitória.

Her throat constricted. *Oh, Yemanjá*, she thought.

"We're here," she croaked, and then cleared her throat. "We're here to keep our community together. We have done no harm to anyone, and are fighting for a place to worship peacefully. We are here for the spirit of Yaya. We want the city of Salvador to know that we can't just be wiped out. We—the children of Xango, Yemanjá, Obatalá and all the orixás—we exist, we are a free people, and we won't be stepped on."

Joaquim clapped and encouraged the crowd to applaud, too.

"Next week, we go to the city officials until they let us worship in our terreiro."

By the day's end, Vitória and the group had stopped by at almost every door in Liberdade. They met barking dogs; they were offered mangoes to eat; they were told to give up; they were embraced.

Vitória asked Joaquim to select four others who were trustworthy and who would go with her to see Senhor Ferreira. At Sister Maria's house, Vitória planned their meeting, serving them juice and sitting in the circle they had formed.

"It's been over a month since we last saw him," said Vitória. "He doesn't like to see us coming over. If we go in a big group, he'll be forced to sit up."

Senhor Ferreira showed up at Sister Maria's house after she, Joaquim, Sister Maria and the four others had turned up at his office. He said they could open the terreiro again, but would have to pay him taxes quarterly. When he was sure they could be trusted with payments, he would pass by twice a year.

"No need to come to my place of work," Senhor Ferreira said. He would come by Sister Maria's to pick up the money.

Vitória wondered if he would soon be asking for whale meat to be cooked for him.

"Thank you, sir," she said, surprised she harboured no ill feeling towards the man. She was just relieved the terreiro was saved.

After he left, she asked Sister Maria if they could prepare a small feast for Yemanjá.

Before she had even finished talking, Sister Maria had herded Vitória to the kitchen. As Vitória hashed a small white onion, Sister Maria boiled corn. They mixed the onions and corn with palm oil, dished it on to a white plate, and placed it in a wicker basket.

They both changed into white dresses and walked down the hill to the main road where trams dashed by. They cut across and went down to the bay, and where the water kissed the shore, they set down the basket. Sister Maria started a hymn to Yemanjá.

"Thank you," Vitória said, pushing the basket into the bay water.

After a day spent dusting windows and benches in the temple, Vitória and Sister Maria arrived home and Baba Sule was sitting across from Sister Maria's pale husband, who had a beer glass in hand.

Vitória knew what Sule's presence meant, and it broke her heart. She had just done something important. Probably the bravest thing she'd ever done in her life and, just like that, she had to leave it behind. She wanted to walk out of the door and run, but her legs led her to the sitting room, where she sat quietly and listened to the words pouring out of Sule's mouth.

"Tereza is ready to receive you. We now have to arrange for travel with an adult heading to Lagos."

"This one is so courageous, she needs no chaperone," said Sister Maria.

Even though the conversation felt like it was taking place above her head, outside of her, still, that was one word Vitória had never thought would be used to describe her.

"Yes, senhora," said Sule, "but she's still a minor. As soon as we find that person, it's back to the motherland."

At almost sixteen, Vitória really didn't want to be treated like a child any more.

"Yaya would be so happy," said Tereza.

Vitória felt herself nodding.

Sister Maria interrogated everyone on their street, looking for Lagos-bound adults. A response came a month later. It was enough time for Vitória to take part in the first ceremony in the newly reopened terreiro. She was so pleased they were celebrating Yemanjá. She didn't know what it was like to dance in Yemanjá's beautiful blue and white robes because she was completely overtaken by the orixá, but after she came out of the trance, she felt better about travelling to Lagos and about leaving behind Joaquim and the terreiro. There was a promise of better ahead. So when

Senhor da Rocha, an acquaintance of Sule's, an older man dressed in a crisp suit and tie, showed up at Sister Maria's, confirming that he'd be making the trip and could go with Vitória, she didn't put up a fight. They were to meet on the quay on 6th June for an afternoon departure.

But she and Joaquim decided to have things go their way for a change.

A day before her travel date, Vitória packed a bag with her clothes, Yaya's sewing kit, money Yaya had left her, her Yemanjá doll, her passport, as well as gari, kola and groundnuts Sister Maria had bought for her journey. It was late morning, and the sun was soft, shaded by clouds that lent the whole place a grey sadness.

Sister Maria was in the garden, washing clothes.

"I'm going now," Vitória said. "Thank you for everything."

"But I'm taking you to the ship," said Sister Maria, wiping the suds off her hands. "Is it today? I could have sworn it was tomorrow. Let me change."

"Yes, it's today, the fifth," said Vitória to Sister Maria's back.

"You're sure you don't want me to come with you?"

"I don't want this goodbye to be sad."

Sister Maria escorted her outside, where Maria's husband was mid laughter, revealing teeth shaped like a rodent's. He barely acknowledged Vitória, but waved at her jauntily and went back to chatting with his friends.

Maria kissed Vitória's cheeks.

"Greet the motherland for me, Bela."

She put in Vitória's hands a lace-wrapped bundle which Vitória realized was money.

"Yaya left it for you to find your sister."

Vitória opened the bundle. She took half of the money and pushed it into Sister Maria's hand before hugging her. "For the terreiro," she said.

Vitória then made her way to Yaya's house, pressed her palms against the orange of its brick and kissed its coolness. Next, she went to Sule, who prayed for her and blessed her journey. She stole around the hill to the three houses on the smaller hill, taking furtive glances over her shoulder. By this time, the sky was shaded purple and orange, with thick clouds. She clapped in front of Joaquim's door, frightened that Sister Maria would pop up behind her.

Joaquim's mother answered and let Vitória in.

"It's your love," the woman said, then laughed nervously. "Sit, my sweet."

"Thank you, mãe," Vitória said, and lowered herself to the lace-covered seat.

If she stayed in Bahia, would this become her home? She already felt as if the walls would cave in and squash her. Figurines sat on every flat surface.

Joaquim appeared from a doorway, and his mother said something to him, ruffled his hair and left them.

Joaquim hugged her. She felt her heart warm.

"Lioness Maria was hard to escape," said Vitória.

"Maria didn't let her own son play with us when he was a boy because she thought we were too rough."

They ate dinner, fish moqueca, then Joaquim walked Vitória outside and up on to the roof, with a sky that hadn't quite cleared but was mottled with clouds that allowed peeks of the stars. Joaquim had spread a cloth on the red brick of the roof and they lay down and looked up. Fireflies darted about, and Joaquim took Vitória's hand and pressed it to his chest. They said nothing for a while, then turned to look at each other.

She was surprised to see his eyes filled with tears.

"Sule told me we wouldn't last long, because you have to find your twin, but the tragedy would have been in never being friends."

She pressed her forehead against his. She could hear his breathing, a quiet whistling—or was it hers? His lips touched hers and she leant into him with all her weight. She hadn't realized how heavy she was, because he fell on his back, and she landed on top of him. They laughed and kissed and cried until sleep stole him away first, and then her.

The sound of birds trilling woke Vitória and, at first, she felt disorientated, with the air whistling about her, with no walls to hem her in, then she let herself be cocooned by Joaquim's arms. He was breathing lightly, his eyelids fluttering. Freckles dotted his nose. He was a beautiful boy. Slowly, she unwound herself from his embrace and looked around. Their neighbourhood was a rich green that covered the different hills around them. Birds swooped up and down, beginning their day. This had been her place of refuge, just as it had been for many before her.

Joaquim stirred and opened his eyes.

"You sleep with your eyes open," he said.

"I don't," she said.

"But I like it. It's like you watch over the world while sleeping. It's beautiful. Vitória, I had the best night I've ever had."

"Me, too."

After breakfast, Vitória hugged Joaquim's mother and thanked her for letting her stay.

Joaquim put on his straw hat, picked up Vitória's basket and took her to the docks.

Senhor da Rocha was already there and he handed Vitória her ticket. He greeted Joaquim with a distant solemn air, but said nothing, so Vitória and Joaquim shifted off away from him, where they could hold hands without being seen.

When the ship's horn tooted, Senhor da Rocha turned immediately to look at them and nodded. They hugged tightly, and when Vitória let go, her stomach knotted. Nervously, she followed Senhor da Rocha up the stairs, holding on to the banister, stiffly looking up, full of regret that she hadn't learnt how to swim. When she arrived at the top, she waved at Joaquim for what felt like a painful eternity. She wanted to be standing on the other side with him. They could live with his mother and when they were both of age, they would get married... It was more secure than what was waiting for her on the other side of the sea.

When the ship finally sailed, Joaquim waved madly and blew kisses at her. Senhor da Rocha told Vitória the women's quarters were downstairs, to the left. She wouldn't see him again until the day the boat docked in Lagos. She wondered if Sister Maria had paid him, but it suited her fine that he left her alone.

The water was calm as the boat went past the small fortress island of São Marcelo and around Itaparica and out of the bay. Then the waves slapped against the ship's sides, choppy and angry. Because she hadn't gone down early enough, she was left with a small berth she had to share with a grim woman who had already chosen the lower bunk.

For the first four days, her belly wouldn't stop emptying itself. The grim woman wouldn't give her the lower bunk, so next to her on the bed Vitória kept her slop bucket, with a stink that made her even sicker. She had to find the strength to take it down before she slept.

When, finally, she felt strong enough, she spent more time above deck, where the crisp air brushed her cheeks. She pondered on Joaquim and Maria, who were black like her, but had been born on the other side of the ocean and would never cross back to see the motherland. She thought also of Yaya, whose ties to both Bahia and Lagos had held strong. If Yaya could have chosen, would she have passed on in Lagos? Where would her spirit go? Were spirits blocked from going back to their land by water? Or did people like her carry them over? These were questions Vitória would probably never find the answers to, so instead she allowed herself to think about how she would find Hassana.

The journey back was worse than the journey away. What had taken her and Yaya just over three weeks lasted for close to three months.

After several storms at sea, and just before the ship drew closer to the African continent, Vitória felt a rush of sorrow. There was no going back to Joaquim; Yaya had left her. She felt so alone it almost angered her. What had she done wrong to have a life that was always tainted by loss? Her father, her mother, siblings, grandmother, Yaya, Joaquim. Anyone she'd ever loved was taken away from her. Wouldn't it be better to not love at all?

CHAPTER EIGHT

Hassana

Every August, the inhabitants of Accra, the Ga people, celebrated Homowo, to mark a moment in their history when, after a long period of famine, the rains began. It was 1897. In Scissors House, the different residents and some of Amerley's aunts had been preparing for weeks.

On the main day of Homowo, Amerley and I walked through Ussher Town and James Town, and when we neared the Ga king's palace, Amerley told me to walk faster. At first, I thought she'd seen John Jr and was avoiding him, but when I looked closer I saw that there were many pairs of people who looked alike. There were twins everywhere. I found myself paralysed. I was at once envious and sad that I couldn't be in the celebration when I belonged there. Amerley muttered sorry and tried to drag me away, but it was too late. I went around looking at the twins, mostly dressed in white. Some identical, others not. My stomach ached. Would I ever find my sister?

Fighting for Private Osman had awoken an energy that had fallen asleep in me, and I became like a dormant volcano just beginning to bubble. I visited him with Hajia, and saw how patients like him were ignored by the asylum staff. I had written the petition and now just had to wait. To fill the space, I started buying even more newspapers. After dinner time with Hajia, I took a lantern outside to read. The reports in the papers had shifted from the British-Asante expedition to the land bills that were threatening to take land away from Africans to give to Europeans. Apart from proposed land-snatching, positions in government that used to go to Africans were now going to Europeans. I couldn't believe how naive I once was, supporting the British army's invasion of Asante. How I wished I could attend the Gold Coast Aborigines' Rights Protection Society's meetings, some of which were open to the public, but they congregated all the way in Cape Coast. They were fiercely opposed to the government's dealings. Luckily, the women in Accra were also beginning to organize themselves, and I wouldn't be left out of *those* meetings.

When the Brazilians first came back to African soil, start-ing in the mid 1830s, the king of the Gas in his hospitality offered them land and many turned these into mango and cashew farms. Amerley's father often said that even though he was a tailor, his heart lived in the soil. They invited me to join them for the weekend at their family farm in Fanofa. We embarked a canoe near the Korle lagoon and were paddled up the Odaw River, where fishermen waved at us, making Amerley and me giggle. After about half an hour, we alighted on an open plain, where the houses numbered four in total. Mr Nelson led us to the house furthest away, under a sun that beat down on us with no mercy. I couldn't wait to be indoors.

We were greeted with the sugary whiff of ripe mangoes hanging low on the many mango trees and rows of green that led to a large two-storey house. A woman shuffled out with three small children tugging on her hem. Amerley ran and threw herself against the woman, who planted kisses all over her. Beaming, Amerley turned to me and waved me over.

"My favourite aunty, Adukoi," she said and talked to her aunt in Ga.

The first thing one noticed about Aunty Adukoi was how straight her hair was. She was dark-skinned, but with hair straight like Rose's and Mrs Ramseyer's.

Mr Nelson hugged his sister and we walked into a house filled with furniture that seemed to have been passed on from five generations ago: it was heavy and stuffy. Mr Nelson quickly changed from his suit and top hat into a light cotton shirt and trousers, then went into the field.

Aunty Adukoi wouldn't let us go outside without first feeding us. She gave us a plate of what I knew of as koose and what Amerley called acarajé, and asked Amerley to tell her more about me.

"Ask her," I heard Amerley say, then she turned to me. "I'll translate for you both."

She clucked through my whole story, then pointed to two of the children. One was a boy and the other a girl.

"My twins," she said. "Very different, but same soul. One calls, the other follows."

"I've been calling," I said. "I'm not sure she's hearing me."

"She has to be ready. But maybe call harder."

It was easy for her to say. I had been calling since I was ten years old. It was now my sixteenth year around the sun, and my sister still had not heeded my call. Wasn't it a sign for me to live my own life?

Over dinner, Aunty Adukoi talked animatedly to her brother. When her eyes enlarged and she made hissing noises, I asked Amerley to translate. Those were the juicy nuggets.

"She said some British people came by," explained Amerley. "They are building a road and their queen allows them to take what they need. Aunty Adukoi said she berated them and kicked them off her land."

"Bului!" Aunty Adukoi shouted. (She'd said, *Bloody fools, all of them*.) Then she turned and smiled at me. "More soup?"

I had to say yes.

I tapped Amerley's shoulder. "Ask your aunty if they came with papers?"

"Yes, some things rolled in their stinky armpits," said Aunty Adukoi. "As if some paper would make me change my mind. This is *our* land. The Ga king gave land to our parents and grandparents."

The snatching of land was no longer just hearsay. It had begun.

We spent the next day helping on the farm, taking out weeds, turning the soil, and plucking mangoes, which Aunty Adukoi would send off to the markets in Accra and as far as Cape Coast. During a break, she brought us calabashes of nmedaa, and rubbed my back as she offered me a third and fourth calabash of the drink. She brought me a bright orange fruit, plump and ready to burst from its ripeness. I bit into it and its juice spilt down my cheeks and down my neck into my blouse. Seconds later, it felt as if the liquid was wringing the life out of my tongue. I squeezed my face and the sensation passed.

I asked Amerley what I was eating but she ignored me.

"Cajou," shouted her aunt.

"Cashew juice never comes out of clothes," Amerley said.

That evening, over another animated discussion, Amerley pinched her face when I asked her to translate.

"It's no different from yesterday," she said.

Even if she was telling the truth, I got the sense that, not used to sharing her aunt's love and adoration, she was sulking at the attention Aunty Adukoi was giving me.

Amerley only brightened up when we got back to Scissors House. I went back to Hajia's house with a basket brimming with cashews and mangoes.

The newspapers were now screaming about the new land ordinance the British colonial government and their queen were threatening to pass. I acquired a copy of the Public Ordinance, thanks to Amerley, who in turn got it from Lawyer Easterman (who still had no news of when Private Osman would be released), and read it from the first leaf to the last, shaking my head at the impunity of the colonial government. It said: *The Director of Works can take any material needed from unoccupied land without compensation being made to any person* and that the governor could declare any unoccupied land an open space. The fines it was threatening to throw at people heated the air in my chest so much that when Amerley found out that the women in Scissors House were having a meeting, I asked Mr Nelson for permission and went to the courtyard to join them.

Gathered around were some of Amerley's aunts, other women who lived in the rooms around Scissors House and many more from the neighbourhood. They asked who would write down the minutes, and I stretched my arm so high I felt my bones pop. They passed me a sheet of paper and an inkpot and pen.

"Our chiefs and headmen and general male population have become enervated and demoralized," one woman started, pacing in the small space left in the courtyard. "They are afraid to speak their minds."

"We escaped slavery in Brazil," another said. "And now we are being made to suffer all over again."

Even though we had gathered because Aunty Adukoi and others like her were dealing with their lands being encroached upon, because the British were taking what they called "wastelands", I relished the energy floating around. I felt in such communion with these women: some, like me, had known what it was like to belong to another human being. What the British were doing was not right. I was protesting because I believed that we could control our own selves. That land belonged in our hands. I was protesting because of Private Osman and how they broke him and were keeping him prisoner in the asylum.

Days later, we slipped on white blouses and wrappers and covered our heads with white scarves. That way, they would see us. I was thrilled and terrified. The women of Ussher Town, Otublohum and all the Ga districts had spilt into the streets. We had compiled our requests and we would leave them with the governor.

We chanted, "No, no, no to these ordinances. We don't want them. Our men don't want them."

We walked up High Street, past Victoriaborg, and stopped in front of Christiansborg, where the government had its offices. The sun shone high above our heads and seemed to be working with the government to drive us away, but we stayed strong, chanting the songs of Amerley's people, shouting, "No, no, no", and clapping our hands. It seemed to take hours before we got a response. A man came out of the castle gate and told us our demands would be heard.

There was also some levity. Amerley and I attended all sorts of events, including one called the Big Entertainment, where women sang and played the piano. I loved singing when I was younger, but hadn't felt brave enough to pursue that talent. Amerley and I sang "Come Birdie Come" for days after, and she encouraged me to sign up to sing at the next Big Entertainment. I would have a whole year to prepare. I considered it, felt inadequate, and decided not to. But when, a week later, Amerley told me about a writing competition for women in the Gold Coast, I didn't hesitate. My younger self would have been surprised about how I'd grown scared of the spotlight. When Husseina and I were in Botu, we sang praise songs with our grandmother and a group of women. I would always be first in line, Husseina hiding behind me. She had the better voice, but I didn't care—I wanted to be seen first. And now I was shrinking from the spotlight, preferring to take part in a contest where no one would see me, only read my words.

I stayed in Amerley's room, hunched over her desk, and wrote the essay all in one sitting. She read it, took a pencil, scratched at it, then passed it back to me. She'd only edited a few punctuation marks—which were never my strong point.

I looked at her and she was smiling.

"You know we're sending this in."

"I'll rewrite it and we can post it."

She insisted on accompanying me to the post office because I kept changing my mind about sending it. Turning around from the post office, on Williams Street there was an open-air studio with a board advertising portraits. I remembered the photographs I'd seen of Mrs Ramseyer and her family. I remembered the photograph of Amerley's mother. I'd taken pictures before, in the mission. Sometimes, Revd Ramseyer assembled all the children to capture us on camera, but I'd never seen a single copy. If I'd had a photograph of Husseina with me, it would probably have helped my longing and loneliness. I ringed Amerley's wrist with my hand and dragged her to the studio. The man, a John Lutterodt lookalike, made us sit in front of a floral curtain, instructing us to wear serious expressions like we had seen in other photographs pinned to the frame. He stood behind a box mounted on a tripod and covered his head with a black cloth, telling us to sit still. I heard a clacking sound, and he lifted the cloth. We only took one photo—I could only afford one, and this wasn't such a novelty for Amerley, so she didn't care. He told us to come back in two weeks to pick up the photograph. It felt like Christmas was coming—I couldn't wait.

"That was John Jr's uncle," said Amerley.

"Blood is strong. They look alike."

"He's a famous photographer. Erick Lutterodt. If you hadn't dragged me in, I would have avoided going there."

"I'm sorry," I said, not realizing that what I'd taken for a lack of enthusiasm was annoyance on Amerley's part. I sulked for a bit, but soon cheered up, because we would have a picture of us for eternity.

Two weeks later, Amerley and I were sitting in the Scissors House courtyard, eating a pawpaw from the tree behind Hajia's house.

"I am marrying John Jr," she said, with the same tone one would use for saying the sky was blue.

A dull ache took hold of my stomach, which I didn't understand. I wasn't the one marrying the man.

"Why?"

"Well, one of my aunts and I had a long conversation, and she's right. I am my father's only child, and this might be the only chance I have at marriage into a good family."

I hoped the aunt wasn't Aunty Adukoi. She seemed too independent and sensible for that. She'd had her children by two different men and she wasn't married to either of their fathers. To be tied to someone you didn't like? I did not see how that could be good for a person. Some of the novels I read described a profound emotion between lovers. The word could not be used to describe Amerley and John Jr. A pit from the pawpaw got stuck between my teeth and wouldn't come out. It irked me, but I needed to talk Amerley out of a bad idea.

"What will you two talk about? Watching you with him is painful."

"I'll have you."

"No, you won't. You're going to live with him and I'll be left alone."

As I said the words, I wondered if I was enraged because of being left alone or if I was genuinely concerned for Amerley. I convinced myself it was the latter.

"He's not so dull. He races horses—and you know I love the races."

"What about school?"

"That's not changing. My aunt said his is the kind of family that can pay to send me to England to learn to be a lady. You know how I like fine things. It's not going to stop me from studying."

No, that wasn't Aunty Adukoi. She couldn't care less about being a lady and European ways. It had to be one of the aunties who made her wear corsets.

"You're already a lady. And why do you want to be European? What about all our protesting against the British?"

"Going to England won't stop me from protesting what they are doing to us. If anything, it will make me understand them more."

While England sounded fascinating, it seemed like the wrong time to be going there. Amerley was being inconsistent.

"Sleep over this. The rest of your life with that bore?"

"It's too late," Amerley said. "The engagement will be held in a month's time."

"If I can be honest, this is not one of your wisest decisions."

Amerley said nothing. The silence grew gnarled and heavy.

"I'm sorry if I was overly blunt."

She said nothing for a while longer, then stood up, placing her hands on her hips.

"I can't be like you. My family expects things of me. You don't have to account to anyone and you don't understand."

"I do understand. I just think you are doing something to please them and it will only end up hurting you. Fight for what *you* want."

"I don't want to talk about this any more. You're wilfully choosing not to understand me and you're annoying me. Not everyone can do whatever it is they want whenever they feel like doing it with no consequences. Most people have someone to account to."

I would have loved to have a mother or aunt to account to. I didn't choose the way my life had ended up. I didn't say anything to Amerley. I simply picked up my bag and the mottled skin of the pawpaw and walked out of the courtyard.

On my way out, I waved at Mr Nelson. I didn't want to tell him about our fight, but he was smiling brightly and flashing a white sheet of paper at me. I took it, thanked him, and walked enough of a distance from their house before ripping open the envelope. My essay had been selected for the competition. I would have to read it in front of an audience, and the top three would be chosen by a panel of judges and awarded handsome prizes. I wanted to run back and tell Amerley, but I decided to steel my heart and self. She was going to do something she didn't believe in just for the good family name, and then she accused me of being rootless. I needed some space from her.

Not speaking to Amerley meant that, after work, instead of walking around with her as she smoked her cigarettes like usual, now I went back to Hajia's house.

That evening, after I washed dishes, Hajia was sitting on a stool, her eyes focused on the sky in the distance. I wondered if she was thinking of her husband. She was so appreciative of how we had written a letter on Private Osman's behalf that her whole demeanour towards me had changed. I told her about being selected for the competition and asked if I could read to her.

"Allah gave you brains," she said, her gold tooth glistening. Her smile had long retreated into her, so I hadn't seen the tooth in a while. "But as they say, some birds run away from water, while ducks search for it. Allah gave you a good head, and he gave me sweet fingers."

It became a ritual. In the afternoons, I would read aloud to Hajia, who, even though she could barely speak English, would tell me to lift my head higher and look people in the eye. She was helpful. I was sure that if she'd been given a chance to learn how to read and count, she would be running many businesses in town.

After we practised one afternoon, she asked me when it was that I'd last dreamt of Husseina. I'd never told her about our dreams. I asked her how she knew.

"Many years ago, when your friend Rose dropped you off to stay with me, she told me about how she thought you needed to stay sad to keep dreaming of your sister. That if your life was peaceful and pain-free, your body would grow comfortable and your soul lazy. You wouldn't do what was needed to find your sister. That's why I was hard on you. When you see the moon, you have to also see its guiding star. I'm sure you only saw me as the moon, but Rose was the guiding star."

I thanked and hugged the woman who had been my ally all along.

"I dream about her all the time," I said. "And then the day I fought with Amerley, I had one of her dreams. She was again surrounded by water and those fluttering sails. She was moving somewhere—I just don't know where to."

"I understand that you don't always want to be sad. To live in constant sadness is not a good way to use your time on this earth."

"And I don't know if it's true that I need to be sad to see her dreams. I am always thinking of her."

"I hope you find her."

"Me, too, Hajia."

I went to Mr Nelson's house but I didn't see Amerley. Her aunts were constantly sending her around to buy this and that. I felt sad that I'd removed myself from my best friend's important milestone, and also that she didn't know about my competition, even if she probably couldn't attend it.

Two days before Amerley's engagement, a day before my competition, Hajia surprised me by asking what she should wear to the engagement. When and how had Amerley come to invite her? She'd managed to avoid me so far—and, admittedly, I her—but she'd somehow made it all the way here to tell Hajia about her engagement. This enraged me. Politely, I told Hajia she should wear nice clothes because Amerley's aunts could be snooty. She asked me what I was wearing and what I wanted to tell her was that I wasn't going, that I would rather wear my nice dress to my essay reading.

"I haven't decided."

That evening, I agonized once more about going to the engagement. I blew hot and cold. I should support my best friend, I told myself, a person who had given me sisterhood, laughter and direction. Then again, she wasn't being true to herself and was making a bad decision. After all that back and forth, I'd wound myself into such a state that I slept and dreamt of the competition, of standing in front of a group of Amerley's aunties heckling me, words refusing to leave my lips. I stood for so long saying nothing that someone had to carry me off the stage. I woke up furious that Amerley was taking up space in my dreams even without physically being in them. Everything was about Amerley. An entire day when Amerley was going to be the centre of attention would be unbearable.

For my reading, Hajia was regal in a beautiful white and blue boubou with a white lace mayafi to veil her head.

"Nana Hajia Shetu the first," I said, and curtsied, pretending I was going to prostrate myself before her, like people did when they met a chief.

"Joker!" said Hajia, and her smile glittered.

Her boys wore shorts and nicely starched shirts. I wore a dress Amerley had given me in spite of not wanting to think about her or have her aura about me. It was the nicest dress I owned. Hajia cast an appraising eye over me, went to her room and returned with a necklace of yellow beads and a vial of kohl, which she uncapped and used to line my eyes. Then she cupped my cheeks and smiled.

The location of the competition was not like I'd pictured in my dreams. In the dream, we sat outside, but in waking life, we filled up a large hall of benches lined in rows. The stage was a small box a few metres higher than the ground, on which stood five wooden chairs with floral upholstery. Next to the stage sat a grim group: two men and a woman. Hajia and the family took their seats and I went up to the front, to a woman wearing white gloves and clutching sheets of papers. She seemed to be in charge. Around her were an older woman and another who looked to be in her twenties. When I approached her and introduced myself, the woman—definitely in charge—ran a finger down her sheet, and when she found my name popped her eyes widely at me and jerked back her head.

"But you're young!" she exclaimed.

She told me to stand next to her while we waited for two others to register. Meanwhile, the room filled up, and my nerves stretched themselves thin with fright. By the time we were told to sit on our floral upholstered seats, I had to hold the chair's surprisingly hard handle to steady the shakes.

We went in alphabetical order, and I went last. The other speeches floated over my head like wisps of clouds, but I took occasional glances at the judges, the grim group I'd seen. Not one smile cracked their faces. One speech went on for too long, and one girl was so nervous she sounded as if she would burst into tears at any minute.

"The next essayist is Hassana Yero."

I stood up, wiped my clammy palms on my hips and went to the small box that was the stage.

"Good morning," I said. Then I remembered Amerley had told me that people loved it when they were also greeted in their language, so I saluted in Ga and then in Hausa. "Min nna nye! Sannunku da zuwa!"

I began: "I learnt how to read in a forest town, after I escaped from my captor."

I narrated my story of escape and how I came to be educated despite it all, and how my education had empowered me to be creative, even when I felt at my wits' end. I talked about finding work on my own, and fighting for an army officer to be treated better. I ended my story by declaring that justice still needed to be served for Private Osman.

I didn't exhale till I was done, and the applause made me bow in spite of the nerves that still coursed through me. Slowly a thrill made its way through my veins, releasing pops of relief and euphoria about me. It was like those days when I opened the scene for my grandmother, but better. There, I was simply a messenger, regurgitating a song that had been passed on to me; here, I was a demiurge—I had strung together words, formed meaning, created something new that people were responding to.

While the judges were deciding on a winner, there was a musical interlude, a young woman playing the flute—not very successfully. I shifted my gaze to the audience and it was brimming out of the hall.

"We have our winners," said the woman judge, getting up and clapping. "In third place is Nancy Tamakloe. A round of applause."

Nancy was the one who had gone on too long. My heart raced. I really wanted to win.

"In second place is Hassana Yero. Miss Yero is our youngest essay writer, so let's encourage her with an enormous round of applause."

The first prize went to the oldest woman. I thought her essay was plain, but as Amerley liked to remind me, in this world of ours, seniority was more important than talent. I wasn't upset for too long, because I won a stationery kit—a fountain pen, a vial of Arnold's green writing ink and some paper—a welcome gift, since I'd depended on Amerley for my writing supplies.

Hajia and her family came up to congratulate me.

"Ah, your mother fed you the head of the malamin bird," said Hajia. "You're too bright!"

As I fought off the image of my mother presenting me with a bowl with a hoopoe's head, the woman in charge pushed by Hajia and rested her gloved fingers on my shoulder. "I was impressed with your essay and your delivery. I'm headmistress of the Wesleyan girls' school. How would you like to teach some young girls? I know it would inspire them to see someone as young as you are be this brilliant."

"I have employment," I said, before I could stop myself.

"Oh, pardon me," she said. "I shouldn't have assumed. I head to Cape Coast on Sunday, the day after tomorrow, so let's discuss this tomorrow. Perhaps I can convince you to consider my offer?"

She drew me a map of how to locate her on one of her sheets.

The next day, Hajia dressed up to go to Amerley's engagement and I told her I would join her after my appointment. I went up Horse Road and made for Victoriaborg, which lay in the opposite direction to Amerley's engagement gathering. I ended up at a whitewashed two-storey house that sat on a wide compound with a balcony wrapped around its second storey and huge trees. When I knocked on the gate, I sparked off frenzied barking. The sound of the beast behind the gate dripped bloodthirstiness.

A girl about my age answered the gate and let me in.

"Shhh, layday," she said, pointing her finger at the brown and white dog, who I was relieved to see tethered to one of the palm trees at the entrance. The girl's pronunciation of *lady* amused and calmed me.

She herded me into the sitting room, airy with high ceilings and windows that fed in a slight breeze. The girl walked up a staircase and came back down trailed by the headmistress, looking more relaxed than the last time I saw her. She wore a long white gown and her hair was pulled into a bun. Her fingers were gloveless.

"Thank you for being punctual," she said.

She told me the work would involve teaching English to primary-school-aged girls in her school. I would also be in charge of their boarding house, making sure the girls kept to the rules and upheld Christian values at every moment of the day.

"You'll have to leave Accra," she concluded. "The school is in Cape Coast."

I felt my belly deflate, as if it were a ball holding my breath. Cape Coast wasn't in my plans. But maybe there was a reason it was coming into my life. It would be a chance to be part of exciting movements like the Native Ladies of Cape Coast and the Gold Coast Aborigines' Rights Protection Society. I took down her address, thanked her, and promised to write to her with an answer.

Then she asked me to stay to dinner. I thought of Amerley's engagement, and accepted her invitation.

When I got back to Hajia's house, she shook her white-veil-covered head.

"Even if you weren't on speaking terms, you don't do what you just did! In this life it's normal to have disagreements, but it's not a reason to disappoint your friend."

Explaining myself to Hajia would make me sound petty, so I said nothing.

"You know she attended your competition?"

"I didn't see her!"

"She left early to prepare for the engagement."

My arms fell limply at my sides. Shame was not a nice emotion. Shame was a dance between pride and contrition. It bounced from anger to sadness to fear and threw you on a loop all over again.

"In any case, I am going to Cape Coast," I blurted out. That was shame talking.

"Well, I hope you make good friends there," said Hajia, pulling off her veil.

In an emotional moment, I had made a decision that had needed time to mature, to be considered. But it was out of my mouth and there was no taking it back. I slept badly that night.

We run by the waterholes. The girls cheer us on. I am far ahead of her, until slowly she takes the lead and, no matter how fast I run, I don't catch up.

I woke up confused. I felt at once out of body and yet strongly pulled to Husseina. Was I being told something about moving to Cape Coast? Was going to Cape Coast taking me further away from Husseina? My brain felt as if it were on fire. I decided to apologize to Amerley, to tell Mr Nelson about my employment offer, and then begin preparations to move to Cape Coast.

A sad look crossed Mr Nelson's face when I told him about moving away. He thanked me for my work and smiled.

"I'll show you how everything is organized," I said, then asked him if Amerley was at home.

"We missed you at the engagement. She's upstairs."

My legs grew heavy as I cut across the courtyard and up the stairs. How would I even bring up how rotten I'd been? I knocked feebly on her door and she opened it. She said nothing, but didn't close the door on me. Clothes were scattered all over the wooden floor.

"Your speech was excellent," she said. "You should have won."

"Thank you," I said, unsure if the time was right to bring up her engagement or if a less volatile subject was needed. *Ask about John Jr*, said my mind. But that was too explosive. So I said, "I've accepted a teaching post in Cape Coast."

She widened her eyes at me as she began to pick clothes off the floor.

"When do you leave?"

"At the year's end."

"It still gives us a month to fight for Private Osman."

I sprang up and hugged her. "Sorry, I was selfish. I should have been there to support you no matter what."

"Well, you'd better not miss my wedding."

"How was the engagement?" I finally grew brave enough to ask.

"I'm not telling you."

"Please!"

"No. Come to the wedding."

Amerley and I sat outside Lawyer Easterman's busy office, watching his clients come and go. We hadn't made an appointment, so his secretary said we'd have to wait for an available slot. We sat on the bench outside his office, under a tree that had more leaves at its roots than on its branches. We spent the time guessing what people had done to need the lawyer's services.

"That one stole someone's goat," said Amerley.

"That one had a big fight with his wife and she slapped him so hard he can't hear," I said—the man held his hand against his cheek the entire time. "He wants his wife to be taught a lesson."

We ended up chortling, to the point that the secretary left her office and came outside to tell us to keep our voices down.

When he could finally see us, Lawyer Easterman led us into his office with a warm hello.

"How is my good friend Mr Nelson?" the lawyer said, slipping off his eyeglasses. "And apologies for not coming to the engagement. Fighting these land ordinances has me coming and going at all hours."

"We understand," said Amerley.

"Now, your case," said Lawyer Easterman, the skin below his eyes creased in sags. "I'm afraid it hasn't moved. The governor wanted to have a few of the inmates released, but the land ordinance issues have taken precedence. You know what I mean…"

"Yes," Amerley and I chorused.

"There must be something we can do," I said. "Should I write another petition?"

"There's nothing stopping you from doing that, but it might not even get read. I'm sorry I don't have better news."

Amerley held my hand all the way to Hajia's house, where we sat on the mats in her sitting room, and I found myself with words stuck in my throat. Amerley told her the bad news.

A few weeks later, I packed my books and clothes into a trunk, feeling bad that I was leaving Hajia alone—Private Osman was still in the asylum. Hajia arranged for a young man in the zongo to carry my trunk to the dock by James Fort, where the steamers had anchored. As I waved good-bye to her and Amerley, I thought of Jane Eyre arriving in Thornfield Hall and I wondered what adventures waited for me at the other end of my journey.

CHAPTER NINE

Vitória

She arrived in Lagos having lost the weight Brazil had wrapped around her body with its moquecas and feijoadas. As per Yaya's dying wishes, Tereza had sold off Yaya's house and bought a new one, smaller than the old house but also an ile petesi, with two storeys.

The first week, Tereza let Vitória sleep. She said she knew how travelling on a ship sucked the life out of a person. The second week, Tereza told Vitória that Yaya's clients would be elated to learn that Yaya's daughter was back and just as good a seamstress. By the third week, it was clear that Vitória didn't want to do anything but stay in bed. She enveloped herself in self-pity and asked Tereza if Yaya would have rejected her if she hadn't been Yemanjá's daughter. Tereza told her she wouldn't have ended up at Yaya's to begin with if it hadn't been for Yemanjá, so it wasn't Yaya who decided anything. It was Yemanjá all along.

Vitória was so deeply enveloped in her sorrow about leaving Bahia and losing Yaya that the only thing that could take her out of it was a shock. Tereza announced that she was going to the Gold Coast to sell beads, fabric and sandals from Brazil, so Vitória would have to go and stay with Senhora dos Santos. Vitória begged her not to go and promised she would look for Yaya's old clients. She even had enough money to live off for a few months. Tereza agreed to stay for two months, after which she left for the Gold Coast. She kept in touch via letters she sent through Senhora dos Santos.

7th January 1898

Dear Vitória,

It was nice to receive your letter and to hear that Senhora dos Santos is kind enough to read and write on your behalf. This time I am writing because I have a suggestion for you. In my trips around the Gold Coast, I've met many people who are interested in keeping alive our traditions and faith but are struggling to create their terreiros. As a child of Yemanjá and Yaya, you are doubly blessed to come and help them establish a terreiro here. Word on your work in Bahia has spread throughout the community, and you will be treated like a royal. Please bring more of my beads with you. My love to Senhora dos Santos. I hope you can get here as fast as possible. Please find my address in the map below.

Yours,

Tereza

Senhora dos Santos finished reading, folded the letter along its creases and slid it back in the envelope.

"You have quite a decision to make, dear Vitória," she said.

Yaya would be proud if Vitória went, and as for Yemanjá, hers was a spirit that was nurturing, so Vitória was sure the Goddess would protect her throughout. She'd been back from Bahia for just over four months and had collected a few clients, mostly friends of Senhora dos Santos who liked her Brazilian sewing, which had allowed her to earn money to add to the nest egg Yaya had bequeathed her. When she wasn't sewing, she attended Candomblé ceremonies in Senhora dos Santos's home. In Lagos she was still seen as Yaya's daughter and hadn't yet been given much of a role in the terreiro. If she was successful in the Gold Coast, it might trickle back to Lagos, and the older mães would allow her to do more in the temple.

"I'll go," Vitória said to Senhora dos Santos.

Two months later, Vitória took a steamer to the Gold Coast. She'd sewn many clothes to save money for the journey. The ride, although short, was choppy and drained Vitória to the point that when she arrived at the port of James Town she didn't even have the energy to lift her trunk and had to pay a boy to carry it for her. Tereza's address was easy to find, and when Vitória arrived there, she slept for what felt like days, recovering from the voyage. Tereza's Accra quarters consisted of one damp room, with walls covered a ghastly brown.

"I'll do what I have to do and go back to Lagos," said Vitória, when she woke up. "This place…" She pointed to the walls.

"It's because it's close to the sea," said Tereza, coughing.

"In Lagos, we live close to the sea, too, but it's not as bad."

After they had bathed and dressed up, Tereza led them down twisty roads abutting mostly small houses. Some of the streets were wider than those of Lagos, but there were none of the impressive buildings of Bahia. The smell of smoked fish was pervasive. They arrived at a small single-storey house and walked in. Apart from a few benches and a stack of two drums in the corner, it was empty, with not even a single decoration on the wall. These people had really forgotten that the temple should be attractive to both the orixás and congregants. Vitória hadn't realized that they didn't have a single thing in place. She had thought she'd come to teach them the use of sacred leaves (which she'd carried aplenty in her trunk) and make suggestions on how to keep the terreiro open, and then she would leave.

She sneezed loudly, which brought out a woman in her fifties. Vitória almost did a double take—she and Sister Maria could have been sisters.

"Ah!" she exclaimed. "This must be the miracle worker. I can't believe Yaya Silvina's children are here in the flesh. Oh, yes, we are in good hands. And you are so beautiful. Bela."

Tereza introduced the woman as Mãe Ribeiro.

She hugged Vitória and said, "We are so glad you came. I feel called to do this work, but life keeps taking me in different directions. Just yesterday, my father fell and I'm the only one he'll let take care of him."

"When do you want to start ceremonies?" Vitória asked, hoping her face didn't betray how much work needed to be done. Excitement began to seep into her chest—now she could show what she was capable of. Yaya had taught her well. "What do you have?"

"Drums. The musical instruments."

Vitória needed to find a market as soon as possible. Fabric would make a world of difference. Fabric to drape on the walls, fabric to make outfits for the orixás.

"Where's the closest market?"

"Tereza, you'll take her? After the zongo there's a good market. Kola, guinea fowl, goats—you name it, you can find it there."

"And material?"

"You can get good woven fabric there. For European fabric, try the Basel Mission. But our budget is small."

It broke Vitória's heart how money was always a problem for their community. She would ask Tereza to donate some beads, and she would also invest some of her money.

After the third night in the single room, Vitória told Tereza she wanted to find better quarters.

"Suffer now, save money for later. You won't be here for too long."

"I can't breathe. There must be somewhere better."

"Yaya didn't build all she did by being extravagant. Remember her house in Bahia?"

Vitória was thrilled by the work she was doing to get the terreiro on its way, but coming home to this room was bringing down her spirit. *Yemanjá*, she prayed, *just lead me where I should be.*

Over the next week, she and Tereza spent enough time outside the room, visiting the zongo market, where she was able to get by with Hausa. Her heart swelled with pride whenever she could bargain just as Yaya had. Whatever price the vendor started with, she divided it into eight, and started from the bottom eighth amount.

"You are vicious," a man selling cowries told her, and she beamed.

She bought white calico and lace to make simple curtains and blouses. She found a woman walking around with shiny muslin, and from her Vitória bought a rainbow of colours. That way, each orixá could be properly celebrated. She bought plants—dwarf palms, mint and striped dracaena—and pots. Tereza was able to sell her beads to passers-by, so she was happy to accompany Vitória everywhere.

But in the evenings, when they had meals in that small room, Vitória tried to not resent Tereza, who she'd thought of as possessing better taste.

Vitória tucked the pots and plants into the corners of the ceremony room. The orixás thrived in nature. The ideal would have been to be in a forest, but in towns like Accra and Lagos they had no choice but to work out of houses like these.

She had to begin sewing. She'd travelled lightly, with a small sewing kit, but to make the skirts, blouses, curtains and drapery, a machine would speed things up.

"Mãe Ribeiro," she said, sticking her head out of the door that led to the courtyard behind the temple. It was bare, the ground covered in recently swept sand.

"Papa, drink it all," Mãe Ribeiro said to her father, grey-haired and seated on the veranda of the courtyard, calabash in his palms. "Yes, Bela?"

"I would like to sew some things. Do you have a machine?"

"Me?" She laughed and hit her thigh. "No. There's a place called Scissors House though. People also call it the Ship. It's green and yellow. Everyone knows it. Go there and ask for Mr Nelson. He's a lovely man—nicer than those women who call themselves seamstresses. I'm sure he'll let you work on his machine. He won't even take your money, but offer it all the same."

Vitória gathered up her fabric, folded it into a basket and left the temple with Mãe Ribeiro, who stopped and stood in the doorway.

"Go left here and keep walking up," Mãe Ribeiro said. "It should be on the right. But ask for Shipemli if you get lost."

Mãe Ribeiro was forgetting that Vitória could only speak Portuguese, Yoruba and Hausa. She needed English and Ga. She found the house easily, so her worries were unfounded. She went through the door under the sign which must have read, *Scissors House*. She'd been in the place before, she felt. It pocked the skin on her arms. Inside, there was a desk, a rack bursting with clothing on hangers. No one was behind the desk. On the wall was a photograph of a Bahiana lady, and Vitória's heart pinched. Would she ever return to Bahia?

The door swung open from behind and she froze. It was like looking in her own face. It was as if she'd just woken up. Or as if a bucket of water had been splashed across her face. As if sleepwalking, she floated to the person, reached out and touched the face across from her, to check if she was awake or if this was a dream. The person across from her stood with her arms at her sides, her lips wide open, and she, too, reached out to her.

"Hassana," Vitória finally exhaled and melted into her sister's arms.

She felt at once at home and outside of it. Strange and yet as if this were the most normal thing. A lump formed in her throat and wouldn't go away. They held each other and only let go when a man cleared his throat.

Hassana spoke to him in rapid English.

His eyes pressed together and he came from behind his desk and hugged them both.

"English?" Hassana asked.

Vitória shook her head. "Portuguese," she said.

"Incredible," said the man, who must have been Mr Nelson, in Portuguese.

Hassana was plumper than her sister, her skin more red than brown. She wore her hair tied up in a bun. These are the details that Vitória soaked herself in when she watched her sister. She imagined Hassana saw in her a slimmer version of herself with brown skin, with hair parted in two cornrows. Two pieces of a whole.

Vitória took Hassana's hands and studied them, incredulous that this day had come—she truly hadn't believed it possible. Deep down, she was sure she'd lost Hassana, and maybe it was why she had always looked to the future and not to the past. She'd arrived in Lagos only six months before and she'd already found her sister. It seemed like a miracle. She wouldn't let go of her sister's hands.

"I came from Cape Coast for my friend's wedding," said Hassana, breaking the trance Vitória had wound herself into. "I can't believe you're here. That this is you." She spoke in Gourmanchéma, but it came out uncertain.

Hassana asked the man something, and he nodded and pointed behind him.

Vitória let herself be led out of the room, into a court-yard hemmed in by other buildings, up a staircase and into a bedroom with a view of the sea.

"How long have you been here?" Hassana asked.

Vitória found her words cushioned so deep in shock and surprise that they chose to stay stuck in her throat. She had to clear her throat.

"Almost two weeks," she said.

Gourmanchéma was a language she hadn't spoken in years. How would they talk to each other in the most comfortable way? The languages that came with ease to Vitória were Portuguese, Yoruba and Hausa, thanks to Sule. Gourmanchéma was a distant song in her ear. She was sure Hassana spoke English and maybe Portuguese, seeing as she was in a community of Brazilians, but it would feel so out of skin to be speaking to each other in a language that was not theirs, one that had been formed so far away from home.

Her sister sat on the bed as if it were her room, pushed to the side the mess of clothing and patted the space by her.

"Are you staying here?" Vitória asked in Hausa. They would switch between Gourmanchéma and Hausa, the way they did when the caravans arrived in Botu.

"No. I was picking up a dress from Mr Nelson. His daughter, my friend, is getting married. This is her room."

Vitória truly felt as if she were staring in a mirror. The last time they had seen each other, Hassana had screamed herself hoarse. Then they were ten. Now they were seventeen. There were many questions, but they kept quiet, each touching the other's cheek. They had to unpack how they had found each other. The overwhelming fragrance of jasmine clogged Vitória's nose.

"You were in Brazil?" Hassana asked.

Vitória nodded. Her words truly were a jumble. Her emotions had tied them in knots all over her belly.

"I dreamt it."

"I know," said Vitória.

Hassana talked rapidly about what her journey had been. She had the gift of language and spoke beautifully, even as she mixed languages. Her voice was a song. Vitória shared some of her story, too. When the sun began to colour the sky in shades of purple and orange, Vitória realized it was getting late and told Hassana she didn't know Accra very well.

"I'll walk back with you. Will you come with me to the wedding tomorrow?" said Hassana.

Vitória nodded. "I have to ask Mr Nelson to use his…" She didn't know the word for *machine* in Hausa or Gourmanchéma, so she said it in Portuguese, and mimed the circular motion of the wheel.

"He's like a father to me. He won't say no. Come."

Vitória picked up her basket and followed Hassana down.

Hassana started speaking, and Vitória cut in. She could tell the man better what she needed.

"Pai," she said, "I am making curtains, some blouses and skirts." She was cautious about telling him that it was for Candomblé ceremonies, because she knew too well that people who were staunchly Catholic condemned them.

"You are welcome here whenever you like."

Vitória had been planning to trace her steps back to the terreiro and then go to Tereza's room from there, but when she explained where Tereza was staying, Hassana knew a quicker route.

They hooked arms and left Scissors House, walking towards the grey sea.

"You were on the other side of this," said Hassana, spreading her five fingers at the sea. "This was separating us."

"But it also brought us back together," said Vitória. The sea was Yemanjá's domain and, while it was true that the sea could be destructive, it was also a source of plenty.

"If only Aminah were here with us," said Hassana.

A sob caught in Vitória's throat, and she stopped and covered her mouth. A rush of joy and sadness and pure euphoria washed over her. She was incredulous that she was in the same place as her sister.

Hassana hugged her, and when Vitória had collected herself, they walked to Tereza's home.

"How I wish you could stay here with me!" Vitória said.

"But it's small, uncomfortable, and smells like unwashed undergarments. And Tereza takes up a lot of space."

Hassana laughed. "And I wish you could come back with me, but I share a room with ground millet. After tomorrow's wedding, we'll make new arrangements."

"Sit with me a while," said Vitória, settling on the stoop in front of Tereza's door. If Tereza was home, the door would have been ajar.

"Even though I told Hajia—the woman I live with—I wouldn't be long, I can't tear myself away."

Hassana sat and laid her head on Vitória's shoulder. Her body was warm and gave off whiffs of talcum powder. As little girls, Vitória was often the one who put her head on Hassana's shoulder.

"Is Hajia good to you?" Vitória asked.

"She's the closest thing to home I've had all these years. Her tuo is almost as good as Na's."

"Tuo!" said Vitória. "I haven't thought of tuo in so long. I would give anything to have a bowl of Na's dried okra and tuo, just for it to run down my arms. You always stole my last piece of meat."

"I promise to give you every last piece of meat of mine from now on," said Hassana. "I'm sure Hajia would be more than pleased to cook for you. And you? Who was the best person you met?"

Vitória told her about Yaya saving her from Baba Kaseko, and Hassana shared her Wofa Sarpong stories.

A man passed by, ringing a bell and carrying a load of yams on his head.

"Do you ever wonder what's happened to Botu? To the people we left behind?" asked Hassana.

"To tell you the truth, I was afraid to think of even you. I don't know if I would have survived if I had thought of home and everyone we lost."

"Sometimes, I wanted to retrace my steps to slit the throats of the people who had kidnapped us, sold us, and bought us."

Vitória laughed. "You haven't changed."

Although, when Hassana talked about teaching in Cape Coast and Vitória watched her sister, she noticed that the words Hassana chose, the way she gestured, talking with her fingers, as if she were picking up invisible morsels of air—those were all new. The face she looked at was so familiar it was as if they hadn't spent any time apart, but some things *had* changed.

"I am so happy," said Hassana, looking up at Vitória. "Can you believe we found each other?"

Vitória shook her head.

They talked some more, clung to each other, and watched the moon climb higher in the sky. It was only when Tereza returned that Hassana said she hadn't realized hours had gone by.

Tereza clasped her mouth and stood rooted in place.

"Hassana, Tereza. Tereza, Hassana, my twin sister."

Tereza hugged Hassana as if she were reunited with an old friend, then she clapped and danced.

When she let go of Hassana, she said, "Now Yaya can rest in peace."

"Tereza must come to the wedding, too," said Hassana. "I am sad to leave you, but I must. May morning meet us."

Vitória stood up and wrapped her arms around Hassana.

Later that evening, Vitória slid out of the musty room and sat on the stoop, while Tereza slept. She finally let her emotions, in their rainbow of colours, flood over her. Here she was, thinking she would finish helping out at the temple and skip back to Lagos. To her sister she was Husseina, not Vitória. Husseina was from a whole lifetime before this one. Each time she wiped away tears, more gushed out. When she'd thought of this day, which she rarely had, she'd imagined the sense of bittersweetness she would experience, but she hadn't expected such deep sadness.

She let a repressed memory surface: the first time they'd slept apart. All these years, Vitória had blamed this for everything that followed. Their father had disappeared; their stepmother had gone to find a suitor for their eldest sister. They'd always slept by their mother, but when they learnt she was carrying another child, they moved in with their grandmother, who would tell them stories and then fall asleep. Her snores were louder than a lion's roar. In those days, their dreams were very similar. They could finish each other's sentences when describing their night stories. Out of the blue, Hassana decided that she wasn't going to sleep with their grandmother any more, and said that Vitória slept with her eyes open and scared her. Hassana moved in with Aminah. Their first separation. That night, Vitória dreamt a dream that paralysed her limbs, kept her in a world haloed with the deepest blue sky, where rivers rushed with the power of horse's hooves, where the sound of a drum echoed for days. Everything grew intense. She fell into a hole and circled downwards into an unending spiral. She was just being pulled under, into its vortex, when Hassana came and dragged her out of the hut. Barely minutes later, waking life became death, too. Horsemen wielding guns gathered them up. Smoke whirled up about them and fire fried the village. She was tied up and kept separate from Hassana, a separation that had led them far apart. Until now.

And now, they hardly spoke the same language. People thought they were special, extraordinary, and Vitória imagined it was because they were the only kinds of people who were brought on to the earth without being lonely. They entered life together, they trod the earth together on paths that were so intertwined they became two in one. And yet life had split them up prematurely, sent them through trying times and shaped them into two different young women, and suddenly they were supposed to pick up from where they had left off?

She wiped her eyes. It was good to have this time to herself. *Yemanjá, Ibeji*, she whispered, *we're together now. Guide us.*

She listened. The night whispered back with the crashing of waves, dogs howling, a man slurring a drunken song. The air smelt like a damp rag. Swampy.

She palmed her cheek and looked at the wisps of cloud floating slowly by the moon. Everyone had pushed her back to her sister. What did *she* want now?

*

Vitória, Hassana and Tereza sat on the third bench in a packed room. It was a beautiful ceremony that filled Vitória's heart with yearning—could she have had this with Joaquim? But finding her sister was, in the end, what she wanted—wasn't it? It bothered her that the answers weren't so easy. She felt joy, yes, but confusion, too. She shoved these difficult thoughts from her mind and focused on the beauty before her.

The bride wore a crêpe de Chine dress with the lightest lace veil. It looked like it had come out of a catalogue. She would love to see how it was put together and copy it for her clients in Lagos.

After the ceremony, whose details escaped her because the priest spoke in Ga and in English, they went to another green and yellow two-storey house. Inside, the drumming made her shuffle her feet even though the music was new. She watched the bride make her way around. The bodice of her dress had two layers of fabric—she would need to try that.

Hassana brought her a plate of the sourest tuo she had tasted in her life.

"I didn't like it either at first, but it's finally grown on me," she said. "It's called kenkey."

It was inedible. Vitória ate only the fried fish and salsa accompanying it.

Mr Nelson came by with a group of friends.

"Two Hassanas!"

"She speaks Portuguese," said Mr Nelson, pressing Vitória's shoulder.

"Hurrah for a Portuguese Hassana!"

Their joy cracked a smile on Vitória's face. She was pleased her sister had also found a community that loved her. She imagined what it would have been like if Hassana had ended up in Bahia. How Yaya would have fussed over the two of them!

"Eat! Drink!" said Mr Nelson, then he whispered something to Hassana.

She went away and came back with a calabash of tree-bark-coloured drink and Vitória tasted it and didn't like it, but took sips to not offend anyone. Hassana led her to a woman with a veil on her head, like women in the Botu caravans and in some parts of Lagos wore.

"This is Husseina," said Hassana.

"Vitória."

Hassana looked taken aback.

"Hajia, this is Vitória."

"Welcome," Hajia said in Hausa, revealing a gold tooth.

"Hajia has been my mother and protector," Hassana said.

"Your sister is very stubborn, but with the softest heart. And such a fighter. Vitória, welcome back. You're my daughter, too."

It wasn't lost on Vitória. How many parents she—they—had gained. That was the orixás, she told herself.

Amerley, the bride, was about the same age as them. When she made her way to them, she palmed Vitória's cheeks with a familiarity that Vitória wasn't sure what to do with. A woman holding a calabash of strong-smelling drink came and pointed at Hassana and her. She drawled something and Hassana nodded.

"Lovely girls," the woman concluded in Portuguese, taking a sip from her calabash and moving on.

Another woman came bounding out of a room downstairs, wiping her arms on her skirt. She had straight hair, like some of the Creoles in Bahia.

"Let me see her," she said in Portuguese, shoving people from her path. "This is beautiful." She clasped her mouth and tears streamed from her eyes.

Vitória hadn't realized how many people had known about them. When she thought of it that way, her heart warmed. The event even began to feel more like a celebration of them than a wedding. Hassana's friend was kind to have the spotlight taken away from her—Vitória would endure more cheek palming if Amerley was *that* generous.

"It would have been a sad story if you hadn't found each other," the woman said, and sobbed. "You finding each other is all of us finding each other."

"Poetic, Aunty Adukoi!" said Amerley.

Hassana didn't let go of her hand.

People kept exclaiming, "Twins!" They said it so often that Vitória learnt the word for *twins* in the Ga language, *haaji*.

The other revellers were too happy in their drinking to be lucid. Drunk people amused her. Their gaits, their expressions, the way they would whip around suddenly to fight with invisible demons. Vitória would rather watch them make fools of themselves than be the attraction, a phenomenon. Growing up in Botu, they hadn't been out of the ordinary. Yes, sometimes when the Sokoto caravan came through, the travellers would make comments about the two-ness of her and her sister, but they were usually having too much fun to care. She didn't want to be constantly thrust into the centre of everyone's gaze. Being reunited with Hassana would do that to her. She watched her sister, still confident, still basking in the attention they were drawing to themselves, but now blanketed with a kind of sorrow and quietness that Vitória understood well. Vitória thought of the Candomblé ceremonies and how they were also spectacles in a way, because people danced in a trance, and those who couldn't receive orixás would watch. When she was the centre of another's gaze in that world, Vitória had never felt unsafe, maybe because she'd been filled with Yemanjá and she hadn't had time to consider shame or being watched. Here, she felt naked, and after Hassana had taken her round yet again, she broke their handhold and went to sit by Tereza.

"You don't look happy," said Tereza.

"I am. It's just… It's overwhelming."

Amerley came by, holding Hassana's hand, and Vitória felt a pang of jealousy.

"Move into my room," said Amerley. "Hassana told me you don't like where you're staying."

Tereza playfully hit Vitória.

Vitória whispered apologies. Tereza was unbothered.

"I'll move into my husband's home. You two should stay here."

"I'll come early tomorrow," Vitória said to Hassana.

"Me, too. Even though I don't want to be a minute apart, I have to get my things from Hajia's house."

Vitória reached for Hassana and said, "Celebrate with your friend today. Tomorrow, I get my sister back." She kissed her sister's cheek.

The next day, Tereza accompanied her to the green and yellow house, carrying Vitória's trunk on her head like a porter. This time, the house stood stately and quiet, stripped of all the marks of the celebrations of the previous day.

"Can you believe I saw this place in my dream? Who knew it would be exactly where we would meet?"

"Eh! Twins, you are powerful," exclaimed Tereza.

They greeted Mr Nelson and cut across the pristine court-yard. One wouldn't have known that just a few hours ago it had revellers and bowls of food and calabashes of drink.

Vitória watched her sister descend the staircase. Hassana was ladylike and wore the airs of someone who hadn't known strife.

"I tried to get here early to clean up," she said, and hugged Vitória and Tereza, who had set the trunk on the ground. "But you're here early, too."

Tereza helped them carry the trunk to Amerley's room, and said she had sales to make. After she left, Vitória paced about Amerley's room, which was not much neater than the day before. The bed was unmade, and clothes poured from the wooden wardrobe. Through the window, she caught sight of the sea. She'd let its waves carry her to the other side, and she'd come back this different person. Yet it was still mysterious and frightening.

Hassana picked up a hat from the floor. "Can you imagine someone else being messier than me?"

Vitória stared at the clothes on the bed. They had to get to know each other again. She lived in Lagos; Hassana lived in Cape Coast. Who would have to move?

"What do you have to do today?" Hassana asked, shattering Vitória's thoughts.

"Sewing. And you?"

"I return to school in three days and I have some stationery to buy."

"I'll come with you. I also need a few more things for my ceremony."

"What ceremony?"

Vitória wasn't sure how her sister would react.

"I'm starting something like a church."

"My sister is a lady of the book?"

"It's different from the Catholic belief. Our faith is about our ancestors who protect us, about the forces of good that live in nature. You should come to our first ceremony. It's the day before you leave."

Hassana shrugged. "I don't know what good religion does anybody. I'll buy you whatever you need though."

"I have money," Vitória retorted. She sounded as if she'd bitten her tongue. She was heaviness itself and Hassana was light, with wings.

Hassana led them out of Scissors House and into the hot air. They wound their way on to a major thoroughfare, and

Hassana pointed to one thing here and another thing there. Vitória barely listened. An idea had come to her. What if she stayed in Accra, to be closer to Hassana? She was ready to try on Accra, as one would new clothes, although it already wasn't fitting right—she couldn't feel it in her bones. She'd arrived in Bahia younger than she was now, but even then she'd had a premonition she could spend quite a bit of time there. One could feel these things. Accra wasn't seeping into her skin the way Lagos and Salvador had though. She was probably thinking too much about it, she told herself, and looked at the street lamp Hassana had pointed out.

"Imagine if we had these in Botu," she said. "We would have stayed up all night getting up to mischief."

Hassana talked about this building, about that shop. When there were no buildings to describe, she told Vitória about how she and the women in Accra had marched up this very road to see the governor.

"In Cape Coast I've joined a women's group. We are fighting there, too, to keep our land in our hands."

Hassana hadn't lost her independent and strong streak.

They arrived at a giant building, from which others were entering and leaving.

"Isn't this impressive?" said Hassana.

Vitória wanted to tell Hassana about the majestic coaches and trams that sped along the streets of Bahia, of which Accra had nothing comparable. And this building looked like a glorified trading post. What would Hassana say to the Elevador Lacerda?

"It is," said Vitória.

"When I first arrived in Accra, I came in here and wanted to run and hide. I couldn't buy anything. Now that I make some money at least I can afford writing supplies. I still can't buy their clothes. I only earn eighteen pounds a year, but you can make me fancy clothes."

"Yes," Vitória said. "But I'm also expensive."

Hassana hooked her arm in Vitória's and they went to the counter and asked for paper, ink, fountain pens and a packet of biscuits. Vitória bought paper (she could fold it into crowns and other shapes for the orixás' costumes), two handheld mirrors (they were too plain for her liking, but she couldn't afford the ornate ones) and white flowers to decorate the temple for Yemanjá.

On their way back to Scissors House, Hassana said, "I'll find out if there's a sewing shop out there in Cape Coast. Maybe you could come and join me there?"

"Or you could find schools here," Vitória said, her words a rush of hot air she couldn't control. She couldn't be the one who always followed—she was no longer that person. Yaya had said she was the older of the two of them. "I was thinking I should stay in Accra. I could continue helping with the temple and maybe find some sewing work with Mr Nelson."

"That's a wonderful idea," said Hassana.

Later that evening, she and Hassana lay on Amerley's bed. What a journey they'd both been on.

"I'm so glad we found each other," said Hassana.

"Me too."

*

217

Mr Nelson was more than happy to have Vitória work with him. She was fast with his lady clients' clothing, and he helped her stitch together the drapery she needed for the terreiro's walls. When she'd laid out the giant skirts she'd made, he stood across from her work and covered his mouth.

"This feels like home," he said, his words getting caught in his tongue.

"We'll be meeting on Friday," Vitória ventured, "if you want to come and join us. Everyone is welcome."

He shook his head no.

"I like seeing this, but I go to church," he said.

She filled the basket with the clothes and drapery and dashed to the temple, where Mãe Ribeiro was practising songs with a small group. She waved at Vitória, who set to work, hanging blue and white fabric on the walls. In this first ceremony Yemanjá would be thanked. She took the paper she'd bought, cut out triangles from its top and then sewed a curtain of beads to the crown.

Vitória bit her nails. Something seemed missing from the room, fragrant with burning mint—more colour or more plants? The walls and ceilings had been covered in palm leaves to welcome the orixás. Tereza told her she'd transformed the temple, and to stop fussing. She went to the courtyard, and made sure the women had prepared more than enough food. Yaya always said it was better to have more. In a room in the back, guinea fowl were ready to be sacrificed. Mãe Ribeiro was beautiful all in white, with red beads draped around her neck.

She went back outside and Hassana walked in.

Vitória dashed to her and told her to sit wherever she liked. "Tereza will take care of you."

When Mãe Ribeiro started singing, Vitória went to the front. For a beat, she wondered what she was doing up there when she wasn't an elder, but she remembered that Yaya had told her that sometimes even children were elders in Candomblé. The room filled up, and soon she saw a sea of white.

"Yemanjá ile," a girl belted out, hushing the crowd.

Vitória's toes tingled.

She folds me into her whirlpool, until my limbs are the water, the water is me, is within me. She has brought me home, and I have brought her home. We dance. We twist. We circle around. Our energy fans out. Gratitude pours into and out of me. I am thankful. And so is she.

When Vitória came to, the congregation had been served with bowls of boiled corn doused in palm oil and pieces of fried guinea fowl. She hugged people who thanked her for finally giving the community a terreiro. She searched for Hassana and found her seated on the floor with Tereza.

"You danced exquisitely," said Hassana, pushing her elbows out and attempting to dance. "And that crown!"

"It was Yemanjá," said Vitória. She sat down and scanned people's faces— everyone appeared content.

*

Back in Amerley's room, Vitória wanted to sink into bed and sleep deeply.

"So you were really possessed?"

"I just receive Yemanjá."

"What does it feel like?"

"I don't know. After she leaves, I'm just left feeling lighter, blessed, happy."

She stared at the wardrobe, bursting open.

"Will she come for her clothes? Amerley?"

"She plans to give them away now that she's a married woman. And she's going to England soon, so she'll return with a new wardrobe."

"Have you been to England?" Vitória asked.

"I've never left the Gold Coast. I almost crossed the sea to find you, but Mr Nelson showed me my ludicrous ways. I knew you were in Brazil. Tell me about it."

Vitória was drained, but she indulged her sister.

"It had everything. Carriages, horses, trams. Buildings that had rooms that moved up and down a hill. It was as if God had brought together all the people in the world and told them to live together. You could find people darker than me; you could find people so pale they were see-through. And usually the darker you were, the poorer you were. It was only ten years ago that they stopped having slaves, so some people were scared of being returned to their owners."

"Even here, if you're not careful you can still be sold. Did you have friends?"

"I had a close friend. Joaquim."

"I don't speak Portuguese, but that sounds like a male name."

Hassana cracked a wide smile. She sat up and clasped her waist theatrically.

"Husseina Yero, you had a gentleman friend?" She clapped. "Here I was, pitying you all this time."

Vitória smiled. She missed him, but most times he slipped her mind. She told Hassana about their trips around Bahia and about what he looked like and their first kiss.

"Did you love him?"

"I liked him a lot."

"If he had seen you tonight, he would have gasped. That crown you made... Even the plain mirrors looked regal."

"It was Yemanjá." Vitória yawned.

"Surely you don't believe that? That was you."

"It's not that different from believing in Otienu."

"I don't believe in Otienu any more."

"You must believe in something."

"Us. I believe in us. We came back together by harnessing our dreams. Christianity, Islam, Otienu... It's all to keep us in line and to give us something outside of ourselves to keep us in check. We—people—can and should look within ourselves. But maybe stick to Otienu. Our belief. I can respect that."

Vitória watched her sister, now standing and holding her waist. Hassana had always been one to not back out of an argument. But Vitória knew in her bones that Yemanjá had watched over them, kept them circulating within the same spheres. That had taken a power that was more than human. It was spirit. But she didn't need to convince a person who didn't want to be convinced. Yemanjá had given her something Otienu hadn't.

"Next time you come to Accra, I'll explain some more. For now I'm exhausted."

The next day, they walked to the port. When they parted, Vitória exhaled, suddenly lighter. Now she could breathe.

CHAPTER TEN
Hassana

I returned to Accra from Cape Coast, my feelings scattered, as if tossed in a corn grinder. I was thrilled to see my sister after five months apart, but I was also filled with anxiety because Vitória was nothing like the Husseina I'd kept in my dreams. The Husseina I'd held on to was quiet but ready to go on whatever adventure I hatched. Yes, many years had gone by and we were now young women and not the little girls we had left behind in Botu, but I wondered if people could change so much. I knew I had grown less spontaneous, developed my own set of fears, but no one could say I was so different from the girl I used to be. I couldn't bring myself to call her Vitória.

I went up to Amerley's room and Husseina wasn't there. The room was familiar and different all at once. Long gone was the fragrance of jasmine. Now the air was crisp, with almost no smell. My sister's smell was neutral. Everything was in its place. No clothes on the floor or on the bed. I went down to Mr Nelson's workshop and there she was, crouched behind a sewing machine. Mr Nelson saw me first and folded me in a great hug. Husseina came behind me and hugged me, too. I felt such a flooding of love.

Mr Nelson said Husseina could take her break and we went into the courtyard. She seemed happy.

"How do you like Mr Nelson?"

"He's funny," she said. "We talk a lot about Bahia. He doesn't have many memories of the place, but still calls it home. He frowns on Candomblé, but still lets me sew for the ceremonies just because it reminds him of Bahia."

"I don't have a place I call home any more."

"Not Cape Coast? Not here?"

I shook my head. "And you?"

"Lagos, I suppose. Even Bahia was home for a stretch."

"You're lucky."

She told me about some of her clients, European women and a sprinkling of African women living in Victoriaborg—African women who wanted to be more European than the Europeans. These African women liked the Brazilian twist she put on clothes, such as her lace appliqués and beading, and she was getting a few orders. Not as many as in Lagos, but enough to keep her busy. She asked me about my students, and I told her about the bright ones who were reading faster than I'd anticipated and those who couldn't speak a word of English. We trod on safe topics, and I held my breath, waiting for her to ask when I was moving to Accra. The truth was, I liked Cape Coast and I wanted her to join me there. Paradoxically, seeing her success with the ladies of Accra encouraged me. If she asked, I would tell her to come and establish her own shop in Cape Coast, with the reputation of Scissors House behind her. But I had to step slowly and softly.

I was excited about being back at the Gold Coast for another reason. It was Homowo season, when the Gas marked the end of hunger, and I could, after all these years of pining for my twin, take Husseina to the celebration of twins. I was sure she would love it.

Husseina cooked a dish with beans and rice and plantains, which Mr Nelson said was just like his mother's cooking. It was nice, but I could have done with bigger chunks of meat. When he and Husseina returned to work, I went up to read. The Wesleyan church sent in books for our school library, and I think I was the only one who went in there. I was working through the second volume of *Great Expectations*, and completely understood Pip's change in fortunes. Except I hadn't come into money—I had found the rest of me.

A few days later, the sound of drumming woke me, and I shook Husseina awake.

"You don't want to miss the beginning of the festival."

"I haven't bathed."

"No one will know. Just throw on a dress."

Husseina reluctantly put on the same dress she'd worn the day before and I dragged her down the stairs and outside.

Everybody had poured out of Scissors House and the neighbouring houses to see the procession go by. We clapped at the men and boys wearing red and black, their skin covered in white chalk. Umbrellas shaded the heads of the Ga king and his entourage, as he grabbed a handful of orange kpokpoi and sprinkled it on the ground.

"What food is that?" Husseina asked.

"Fresh ground corn that's been steamed and cooked with palm soup and fish. It's celebrating the end of hunger. When the Gas first arrived here, they suffered from a huge famine and when the rains began again, this was their way of thanking the ancestors for helping them. *Homo* is *hunger*. And *wo* is *making fun of*."

"Just like Carnaval," Husseina said. "And just like Candomblé. This should make you believe in what I do." I was happy to see this pleased her. "It's like in Bahia when we would leave food for the ancestors and the orixás at crossroads."

Later that day, Amerley invited us to her home. Husseina and I walked past James Fort and just before the red and white lighthouse made a left to arrive at the Lutterodt family home. The courtyard was teeming with people, who kept exclaiming, "Haaji!" every time they saw us. It amused me so much that I decided to start counting the number of people who said it.

"This is annoying," Husseina said under her breath in Gourmanchéma. She could have shouted out the words and people would have had no clue.

Amerley was passing around plates of yellow kpokpoi drowned in palm soup. It was one of my favourite times of the year, and the day felt very special because we got to eat something that was only made once a year.

Aunty Adukoi called us over and wrapped us both in her arms. Her own twins ran to hug us.

"Are you going to the twin celebration?" asked the

226

younger twin, the girl. I saw myself in her, even though in our case I was older. The boy was brooding, like Husseina.

Amerley, free of her plates, came to join us in Aunty Adukoi's circle. In just three months of being married, her face had puffed up. My friend's clothes swallowed her frame. She didn't seem as put together as she used to be. She was never a sharp dresser like Husseina was, but she was creative, and used to be the kind of person who drew attention to herself. Now she appeared regular. And tired.

"How long are you staying?" she asked me.

"Why?" I said.

"I have news about our case."

"When is the baby coming?" an aunt shouted at her and laughed, rattling off something in Ga, and then grabbing her own belly. "Talking about cases when this is more important!"

I felt bad for Amerley. The glamour of being a new bride was already fading and now she was expected to become a mother. I couldn't imagine being mother to anyone. My life was just starting. We were only seventeen. But I supposed my mother had had my elder sister when she was much younger. I tried to put on a brave smile for Amerley. At least she was still going to school.

"Patience, Aunty Naa," she said. Then she turned to me and said, "Lawyer Easterman said the one person he could have counted on to free Private Osman has been relieved of his post."

"And who is that person?"

"Dr Easmon. He was chief medical officer here in the Gold Coast, originally from Sierra Leone. The government claims he owned a dissident newspaper, and that public officials like him shouldn't have private businesses. Easterman says he was framed, and says it happened just as he was arranging for us to meet him."

"It's so easy for him to say that now," I said, sitting down. I turned to Husseina and explained. "He sat on our case for too long. It wasn't important to him. Poor Hajia. People in Accra just accept nonsense. You should see how fiery people are in Cape Coast."

"In Lagos, too," said Husseina.

"I said the same thing to him, that he wasn't pushing hard like the ARPS people. He said those people are far away from the governor and don't risk losing their situations. I'll try my best to keep working on it," said Amerley. "But I have school and John Jr, so there's only so much time left for me to do other things. And what's *your* plan?"

Her eyes were trained on me.

I shook my head, as if I hadn't heard her even though her words had been as crisp as a bell tolling from a church. She needed to drop the subject.

"Is Vitória moving or are we to expect you back in Accra? I miss having you around."

My arms itched. "Mmm," I said, putting a fistful of kpokpoi into my mouth. I mumbled, "I'm still looking for work here."

I told myself to calm down. Husseina didn't understand English anyway.

The big topic on everyone's lips was how the Asante had started moving en masse to Sierra Leone to pay respects to the Asantehene. The British were worried they would find a way to smuggle back their troublesome king. I admired the Asante spirit. Fighters to the end. It wasn't lost on me that it was because of this fight with the Asante that Private Osman was languishing in that wretched asylum.

After lunch, a lull descended and nobody wanted to move. Flies landed on skin and were barely swatted away. People who were lucky enough to get benches spread themselves supine. Husseina and I went back to Scissors House to rest before the twin festival. I tried to work up some excitement after the discouraging news of Private Osman.

"Do you intend to move back here?" Husseina asked when we returned to the room. My sister, as quiet as she was, could perceive things even in other languages.

"Come to Cape Coast," I said. I sounded authoritative and cold, not the way I'd practised: "*You would greatly improve the sewing culture in Cape Coast.*" Or: "*It's a smaller town, and there are many schools where you can learn English.*" Or: "*You'd like the ladies of Cape Coast—they remind me of you.*" And many other permutations.

She didn't say anything, and I wondered why her way of operating was keeping her feelings buried in her chest. But I wasn't going to start a fight. I would let her stew over what I'd told her and when she was ready to talk I would present her with my convincing arguments.

Being away in Cape Coast, I had been able to ignore a sentiment that had come right back now that we were together. We had grown into completely different people whose only connection—even if it was a strong one—seemed to be being carried in the same womb at the same time. Our paths had diverged and there was nothing left chaining us together except for the accident of our birth. In Cape Coast, I had buried this fear and the nausea that accompanied it, and chosen to look forward to the day when we'd see each other again. I hadn't realized that the delaying game was just me lying to myself.

Husseina slept. Or maybe she was pretending to sleep. I tossed and turned until I fell asleep, too.

We are seated in a carriage, dressed sharply. The horses' hooves clack against a cobblestoned road. Through the window, a man with a top hat drives the horses. We are whipping by tall brown grass. Botu. A baobab tree breaks the sea of brown.

"I'm getting off here," Husseina says, and doesn't turn back to look at me.

The carriage continues moving and all I can do is watch Husseina get smaller and smaller, till she's a dot. The horizon swallows her.

The dream niggled at my brain when we slipped on the white dresses Husseina had sewn us for the twin ceremony. I couldn't get it out of my mind as we walked down the street. I tried to take quick glances at Husseina to find out if she'd dreamt the same thing, but nothing on her face gave away her thoughts. I couldn't read her mind.

It was only at the festival of twins that the heaviness around my chest lifted. There were so many of us, I felt seen. Husseina smiled and gave my hand a squeeze when I slid my fingers between hers. We skipped by old men, mothers carrying two babies in their arms, younger people wearing European jackets, others in batakari. Everything was magnified by two. Even the music seemed louder. We danced through the wide streets of Horse Road and twisted down Hansen Road. Women had set up at the sides of the thoroughfare selling roasted corn and nmedaa. I was sure Hajia was in there somewhere, but there were too many people.

"Awo awo awooo!" shouted many voices. "Aaaba ei!"

"What does it mean?" said Husseina.

"It means they are coming."

"Who are they—"

People carrying liquid- and leaf-filled bowls on their heads tottered forward, as if in a trance or as if ready to attack. They marched in the direction of the sea, trailed by a crowd. Husseina watched them until they were out of sight.

"They have received a spirit," she said quietly.

I bought us roasted corn, and we stopped to eat them. Across from where we stood was a small enclosure of woven palm fronds.

"Let's go here," said Husseina, eyes fixed on the enclosure, as if she'd suddenly gone into a trance of her own.

Inside sat a woman dressed in white and covered in circles of chalk. I was ready to walk out right away, but Husseina did the strangest thing. She sat down and patted the ground next to me.

"Ask her if the spirits are happy with us now."

My Ga was horrendous and I wasn't sure the woman spoke English. I fished for words and didn't even know how to say *spirit*.

"How can I help?" the woman asked in Hausa, and I sighed in relief.

"Please read our shells," Husseina said, holding her corncob like a cudgel.

The lady picked up a number of cowries and shook them in her palms. She tossed them on the dust before her and rocked forwards and backwards. She stared at me.

"You call. She follows. But she is older. You are like the snake biting its tail. If you don't call, she won't follow. And if she doesn't command, you won't call. If you don't call, your sister is lost in her world. If your sister is not searching, you won't call."

I looked at my knees, now covered in the red sand of the stall. I should have discouraged this nonsense. What did it mean and did Husseina believe any of it?

"And one more thing. Your separation has changed you. Cleanse yourselves."

Then the lady shook and didn't say any more.

We walked out.

"That was odd," I said.

"Why?"

"I didn't understand a word."

"What was difficult to understand? She doesn't know anything about us and yet she mentioned our separation."

"Luck," I whispered.

"Remember the tchiluomo bird?"

"The hornbill, the English call them."

"Well, that's exactly what the woman was saying. Remember how one calls and the other follows?"

"I used to say that was us. But I was wrong. They aren't twins—they are male and female. It's a bird and her lover."

What I didn't say to Husseina was that what sounded most ludicrous was that Husseina commanded me. I didn't do anything I didn't want to do and, to be honest, Husseina did very little commanding. The woman's shell reading annoyed me, and Husseina seemed to be gloating in it.

"Let's do the cleansing," she said.

"We'll have to find out where it will take place," I said, with no intention of doing so. More people were heading towards the sea, or the Korle lagoon, where they would pour herbal concoctions into the lagoon to get the blessings of its resident spirit. The cleansing would most likely take place over there. "There are so many people here, I wonder how they plan to get everyone cleansed."

The ceremony seemed sadder after the reading, and that, combined with the news that Private Osman's case hadn't progressed and the dream I'd had, tied my stomach in knots. Something was about to go wrong. I just didn't know what. Or when.

"Ask him," Husseina said.

I turned to the old man she'd suggested and asked him.

"The beach," he said, pointing to a direction I knew was not the beach.

"He says the beach, but Accra is a beach. It could be any-where."

"Ask somebody else."

"Husseina, I'm not going to spend my afternoon asking people who will only send us the wrong way. And besides, why are we listening to a quack?"

"She wasn't a quack."

"She is just exploiting the numbers of people here, and the fact that people think of twins as more than human. But we are no different from other people who are made of flesh and blood. It's just that our mother's body happened to split us in two."

"We *are* different," Husseina said, with a flash of some-thing I'd seen in the eyes of Mrs Ramseyer when she prayed in the mission house. *Fervour* was the word. She truly believed her prayers would make the natives leave their old idols and believe in her God. Well, here I was, well and truly agnostic. "Most people don't have shared dreams."

"They could have been pure coincidence," I said.

"They led me to you. Yemanjá and our dreams."

"Serendipity."

Husseina shook her head.

The chatter of voices grew louder. Some people sang; others slurred their alcohol-charged words; babies cried. I didn't want to be there any more.

"Let's go back to Scissors House," I said. "Sit down and have a proper conversation."

"Have you looked for work here?" she asked. "I decided

not to go back to Lagos to be closer to you, but you haven't done a thing about moving to Accra."

"This isn't the place—"

"Answer me!"

"I would like you to come to Cape Coast. Come and open your own Scissors House there."

She was quiet. Then she said, "You are not in control of my life. I've lived all this time without you and I have thrived. Maybe you are right—we aren't special, and we aren't different. Let's go on living our own lives separately."

My heart sank into my stomach. I took her hands.

"Tell me what you want me to do," I said, searching her eyes.

People bumped into us. I didn't want the carriage dream to manifest.

"The terreiro is running nicely—my work here is done. I'll finish my orders with Mr Nelson and return to Lagos," she said. If only I could drown out the crowd. "I don't speak the language here, and I am not going to start all over again in Cape Coast."

"Let's sleep on this."

"I am not changing my mind."

For many years, I'd imagined coming to this festival of twins with Husseina's arms laced in mine. And here we were, separating from each other in a place that was celebrating our union.

"Please," I said. "*I* can't live without you."

"You already live without me."

When had my sweet sensitive sister grown so cold?

An old lady rushed to us and shouted in Ga that we were conjuring bad spirits into the ceremony.

"Go away!" she shouted. "You're supposed to be blessing us, not cursing us. These are bad ones!" Her voice, although raspy, was being heard by others. Others turned to look at us. "Go away!"

Her words roused hostility in others. Someone picked up a stone. I took Husseina's hand and we ran through the crowd. I felt the stone graze my shoulder.

Outside Scissors House, we panted. It was a moment that should have made us cackle like wild hens. I smiled, but Husseina wouldn't smile back.

A heavy quiet hushed on the room when we got upstairs, and I tried to lighten the mood by humming a song from the twin festival.

"Please don't do that," she said.

"Is this how you always are?" I snapped. "We've all been through horrible things, but we don't wear them on our sleeves. Cheer up."

"I am the way I am. I've always been this way. And you think you're so perfect because you've become European and adopted their ways of talking? Our ways are important, too. I wanted to do the cleansing today, but you picked a fight with me and we got chased out of a beautiful ceremony. Our religions teach us to be one with everything around us. When we celebrate the lagoons, they don't flood and kill us. When we celebrate the earth, she blesses us with good food and abundance. You and me, we are special because we are

236

abundance itself, and we show the world what is possible." She had spoken with so much force, her voice croaked. "But I can't force you to believe. To make myself believe, I had to make myself a vessel to be filled, then I learnt to let go."

I didn't know what she was talking about and pride took the upper hand, so I said, "You can still believe in all these things and not be so… so Pecksniffian! So stuffy. Your Mãe Ribeiro is as light as a butterfly."

"It's your fault all this started," she said, her voice a whisper.

"What do you mean?"

"You're the one who abandoned us. When we slept apart, it invited bad things to our family."

I laughed. "You don't believe that. Those horsemen would have come whether we slept apart or together. We had nothing to do with them. Grow up, Husseina."

"Vitória."

"Oh, for heavens sake! This business of calling yourself Vitória is ludicrous."

She clammed up and didn't speak to me for the rest of the evening.

Husseina woke up before me and when I got downstairs, Mr Nelson had one hand on his hip.

"I'm losing my best seamstress," he said sadly. "Convince her to stay."

"I tried," I said.

Mr Nelson asked me to accompany her to the Elder Dempster office to order her ticket.

"*I have the power to keep you here*," I toyed with telling her, but as soon as I thought the words, I remembered the history of our family: my life on Wofa Sarpong's farm, hers in the Baba man's house in Lagos. Holding her hostage would have been the worst thing I could do to her.

"You can still stay here," I said on the day of her departure. "I'll stop teaching and move in with you, take my time to find something in Accra."

"Accra is not the place for me," she said with the finality of one who would not budge.

"I feel like I've failed."

She said nothing and walked towards the canoe that was filling up.

"We both need time to think," she said. "I will send you a letter."

Her last words irked me. It was clear she had completely imbibed the "One calls, the other follows" words of the soothsayer. As I watched her in the canoe rowing towards the huge ship, I realized that my dream about the horse was playing out before me. My sister was my home, and my home was leaving me again. And she was right about one thing: our dreams were real, and they were the tissue that connected our desires with our waking lives, gave legs to our fears.

When I got back to Scissors House, Mr Nelson beamed at me. I wondered why he was so happy when I'd just been split up from my sister again.

"Bad news and good news like to travel together," he said.

"What do you mean?" I asked.

"Lawyer Easterman sent a messenger to tell you that Private Osman is getting released in a week."

I clapped. At least one thing in my life was going well. I had to go and see Hajia.

Hajia's gold tooth flashed and she buried her head in her veil and muffled a sob.

"Thank you, my daughter," she said. "May Allah reward you. May Allah give you riches upon riches. May Allah bless you."

I told her that Husseina had left for Lagos.

"The problem is that I don't know what to believe," I said. "And she believes in magic. It's hard to work together."

"Everyone believes in magic," said Hajia. "In Islam, we have djinns. The Christians, they believe a man came back from the dead. Even you people who think you don't believe, you believe in your brains. If your sister has this power of connection and commanding, listen to her. That's her strength." Hajia pointed to her heart. "Yours," she said, "is here." She pointed to her head. "Quantity makes cotton draw the stone."

"I don't understand, Hajia."

"Your differences unite you."

Mr and Mrs Ramseyer had sold their religion as clean and rational, but it was true that, deep down, theirs was also one of belief in miracles and magic. And I found it hard, near impossible, to believe in a man who had come from so far away from me, whose death was to save my soul from its love of sin. At least Husseina was proposing

239

a belief that came from soil that I knew. I should give her a chance, but was it too late now?

"She said she would write me a letter," I told Hajia.

"You've forgotten your power."

"What is it?"

"You are the caller. Call out to her."

I asked her how she would cope if Private Osman was worse.

"My grandmother cared for a lot of mad people," she said. "When I was a girl, I used to pray that I would turn mad, because they were the freest people. They were fearless, showing off every part of their bodies, living for days and weeks without a drop of water. And people learnt to leave them alone. They ate, danced, slept wherever they pleased. It taught me that madness was not a crime. Even if my husband gets so bad he has to roam the streets, I would let him. He would always know that this is where home is. He would eat here and be free, not be locked up as if he had killed someone. This happened for us to see that the white man's ways aren't always the best. Thank you for all you've done."

I called out to Husseina as Hajia suggested, but only after I'd been in Cape Coast for a month. I gave myself time to slip back into my life before Husseina was in it. At first, I thought it was going well. I would hold inspections with the girls in the mornings, teach my classes, join the other teachers in the evenings for meals, go to my room or to the library, and life would go on. After the third week, a

240

sense of purposelessness set in. I enjoyed teaching, but I felt lonely. Amerley had told me to find a male companion, but it would have meant going to the boys' school to meet the teachers there, and that didn't appeal to me. I missed Husseina, even with all her introspection. I missed goading her. I had to go home.

22nd September 1898

Dear sister,

I have thought a lot about our last days in Accra, and I'm sorry. I'm ready to try again. I want to know who Vitória is, who Husseina became. You are right, we have become different people, but the truth is that we were always different yet we make a whole. The Chinese have an ancient philosophy of yin and yang. One comma is white and the other is black and together they make a whole, complementing each other. If your clairvoyant lady was right, this is me calling out to you. I hope you send your command my way.

I truly miss you.

Hassana

Sending letters was always an exercise in faith. I wasn't sure my letter would arrive safely in Lagos or how long it would take, and I wasn't sure if Husseina's response would arrive, but three months later, I received a letter. I took the envelope and tore it open with shaky hands. Knowing my sister, it could be anything. She could decide she wanted nothing at all to do with me.

CHAPTER ELEVEN
Vitória/Husseina

She wore a dress that they each owned, which she'd stitched out of purple cotton Tereza had given her and matching lace collars she'd woven while she lived with Sister Maria. She refused Tereza's offers to accompany her. The tingling in her fingers wouldn't go away, and neither would the tightness in her ribs and chest. Hassana's steamer wasn't due till about nine, but she didn't want to be late, didn't want Hassana to have a moment in which she wasn't comfortable, so Vitória arrived at the Lagos sandbar when the sun was only just beginning to rise, with small soft brushes of red and purple around its orange halo. She wanted to extend the warmest of welcomes to make Hassana stay. Part of her own discomfort with the Gold Coast stemmed from that horrible room Tereza had rented when she'd first arrived there.

Others joined her on the shore, some peddling boiled corn, akara and coconuts. Others searched the sea, eager to receive their loved ones. A customs officer in his black uniform and gold buttons sat at a desk, studying his fingernails. She bought herself a coconut and poured its water

242

down her throat. From the distance, a dot appeared and grew larger and larger. Some on the shore clapped their excitement at seeing the steamer.

Vitória waited, impatience scratching at her innards. Did Hassana get as seasick as she did? She was sure her sister wouldn't succumb to such weakness. As she stood there, her palms wet and tingly, a sad memory floated into her mind. The days when she, Hassana and their big sister Aminah scoured the Sokoto caravan for their father. Every day, they weaved through the caravan's people and livestock, looking for Baba and his albino donkey. They never found him, and she wondered if it was one of those mysteries life had thrown her that she would never understand. Suddenly, she panicked. What if Hassana wasn't on the boat?

When she saw Kru men rowing up to the level of the ship's hull, she straightened her back, trying to conjure only good things. "Yemanjá," she whispered, "bring her to me."

People disembarked, descending the rope staircase and climbing into the small branch boats waiting for them. It was easier climbing up than climbing down. Climbing down, she always thought she would miss the branch boat and fall into the water.

The steamer was too far away to see clearly, even though the sun had floated higher up into a clear blue sky, surprising for this time of year. The water looked blue, reminding her of the way the water shone in Bahia. The only separation now between her and Hassana was the deep blue of the sea.

The first boat filled up with people and rowed its way to the shore, and right then passengers descended into the second boat. As the Kru men pulled their branch boat close to the shore, hawkers rushed to the new arrivals; some even got into the sea. Vitória didn't want to be trampled on. She was also sure that Hassana would have waved as soon as she made her way out on to the shore. To her left, a man dressed in rags stood on an upturned boat on the sand and began to raise his arms up and down and to the left and right, directing the branch boat. She'd spent so much time searching the first boat and looking at the man guiding it that she hadn't noticed that the second boat had already been filled.

Voices rose. The crowd doubled and people milled about in—Vitória now realized—frenzied panic.

"The boat has capsized!" somebody said, his voice booming above the others.

The branch boat was floating like an upside-down bowl in the sea, and people were swimming back to the ship, their arms frothing up the water. Some climbed up the rope; others were pulled back into the foaming water below.

Her recurrent nightmare flooded her mind and she was sure, with every single bone in her, that Hassana was in the water. She shook herself back and forth.

"Oh Yemanjá," she hummed. "Oh, Yemanjá." She rocked side to side, singing songs to the spirit who protected twins and mothers and children. Her body eddied, swayed. "Yemanjá protect us. Yemanjá watch over us."

She is shoved into the water, and she whirls, sucked into a funnel. She is tugged down, water whooshing around her,

*until suddenly the whirlpool grows still. She is buoyed up by
the water, even though it is clearly still moving around her.
She doesn't need to sing any more. The song is in her, in her
chest. She is protected by Yemanjá, lady of the water. She took
the children of Xango and Oxum and protected them.*

*"This is your home," a voice says. "You can stay here. Here,
all fear disappears."*

*She sheds her fear, is now drawn to the seductive calm of the
voice. She is at peace. Her fear cowers off and is sucked into
the vortex. Everything she's known and experienced—life in
Botu, being kidnapped, being a slave, running away, living
in Abetifi, moving to Accra—slips into the hole.*

*But these aren't her memories; this isn't her dying. These
are her sister's dreams.*

Hassana is drowning.

*She summons her strength and says, "Yemanjá, Ibeji, we
celebrate you, but we are not ready to join you."*

"Prove it," the voice says, sweet but firm.

*She searches for images. They are in Botu, sitting in their
grandmother's room, singing and laughing till their sides
ache. They are at the waterhole—she dips her feet, Hassana
swims. They sing and sell food to the caravans.*

*"That's all past," says the voice. "You've lived that. It is
what you do with the future that counts."*

Vitória presses her eyes tighter.

*For her sister, she will breathe life into Husseina again.
She won't forget the past, which holds the bricks to build
their future. She pictures this future. She takes Hassana to
Senhora dos Santos, who gives Hassana keys to a school. She*

and Hassana walk hand in hand up and down Bamgbose Street. In her free arm, she is holding a basket of clothing; Hassana is holding books. They sit on a mat at the sea, thanking Yemanjá, watching the wave of people coming and going. They take a photograph together. They are different, but they are together. The future has her sister in it. She wants to live. She wants her sister to live, too.

Yemanjá, make us whole. Yemanjá, make us whole. We want to be made whole. Yemanjá, give us life. Yemanjá, we will always be with you. Keep us safe.

Vitória came to, drenched and breathless, with her feet in the water. How had she gone into the water? Did she swim? She thought she'd been standing on the shore, holding her breath the entire time. How long had she been in the trance?

She exhaled, caught her breath and saw that, just at arm's length, Hassana was lying on the sand, waves crashing next to her feet. She was coughing, struggling to breathe. Vitória knelt down and dug in the sand around Hassana's shoulders, enough so she could slide her arm under Hassana's back. She held her sister up and tapped on her back, until Hassana exhaled deeply. Vitória gave her a big hug. Hassana tried to speak, but Vitória shushed her.

"Welcome home," said Vitória.

Hassana's chest heaved and she broke into giant sobs. Waves washed in and out, lapping at their skirts with what felt like kisses. Vitória reached over and dug the pads of her fingers into the wet sand, until a foamy wave crept under her fingers. *Thank you.*

246

"Let's go home," Hassana said, sucking in a sob, and let Vitória help her up.

The sea, which only a minute ago had caressed Vitória's fingers like a lover, was spitting out bodies. Lifeless bodies. A crate crashed on to the shore in shards. There were other items, too—a boot, a gold plate and a white bust of a man's head—which rolled up on the sand.

Vitória pressed Hassana's shivering body closer to hers and rubbed her arm. She led Hassana along the unending stretch of beach, with the sea on the left, and a network of mangrove bushes on the right.

"*Thank you, Yemanjá,*" she repeated under her breath, as she stole glances at the sea with awe and wonder.

Now she knew. Yemanjá would protect her, no matter what. She had gone into the water and come out. She had gone into the water and saved her sister. Suddenly, she felt lighter. That was the cleansing she'd needed.

"It's good I didn't bring luggage," joked Hassana, as they approached the crossing over to Lagos Island. They had walked for half an hour.

Vitória laughed. "I would have hired a porter to carry your things. What did you bring with you?"

"Some clothes. Mostly books."

Vitória pictured Hassana's books and clothing fluttering to the bottom of the ocean like old forgotten leaves. "I'm sorry, Hassana."

"Better them than my life."

Fear took hold of Vitória's knees as she herded Hassana towards a man in a canoe. She could hear the labouring

247

of her breath. *Yemanjá watches over us*, she calmed herself and lifted herself into the canoe. Hassana climbed in and sat behind Vitória.

"So much water where you live," she said.

Vitória sat stiffly, but nodded. It wasn't until they reached the shore at Lagos Island that she turned around. She still needed to build her confidence in Yemanjá. Hassana, who had nearly drowned, looked wet but unruffled.

On Lagos Island, they walked slowly, while other pedestrians and go-carts and horse carts sped by. They went past the racecourse and arrived at Bamgbose Street. Vitória would have loved to hear her sister's thoughts of Lagos, but she hurried them inside the house, where Tereza shouted a happy welcome from upstairs.

"Thank you," Hassana rasped.

Tereza came down. "What happened?"

"Please boil us some hot water," Vitória said. "We'll tell you everything after we're changed and dry."

Tereza poured the hot water into a metal basin and left the twins in the washroom. Vitória fetched tepid water from a big terracotta pot next to the basin and added it to the hot water. She undid the laces of Hassana's bodice, sloughed off their wet heavy clothes, led her sister into the basin and lathered her with soap. She rinsed away the salt and sand, and combed out Hassana's cornrows. She massaged her sister with shea butter and brought in dry clothes. Then she bathed herself.

"If you want to sleep before we eat, let us know. Your room is upstairs."

"Thank you, Huss—Vitó…"

"Husseina."

Tereza had prepared the table Yaya used for special occasions. Laid out on the white tablecloth were the best plates and crockery they owned, shipped from Bahia.

Husseina could tell Tereza was impatient—her mouth kept twitching—but she said nothing, and instead dished out stewed vegetables and boiled yam on to their plates. They ate silently, the clinks of the forks hitting their plates the only sound in the dining room.

"So?" said Tereza so suddenly that Husseina almost laughed.

Husseina wiped her lips and set her fork and knife at the edge of her plate, just as Tereza had taught her when she'd first arrived in Yaya's home.

"She almost drowned."

"Ay, Xango," said Tereza. "What happened?"

"I went down the rope ladder and entered the branch boat, with my bag of belongings," Hassana said in Hausa and in English, for Tereza's benefit. Her chest of books and clothing were lowered in after her. Other passengers came down, but one man had five trunks and insisted they all had to come into the branch boat. The other passengers protested, said the boat was already full, but the man insisted that he'd had too many things stolen the last time he'd left his possessions idling.

"I told him to take the next boat, and he called me an insolent girl. The irate man refused to give up and the Kru men squeezed in the man and his trunks. As they were

249

rowing towards the shore, the boat tipped over and we were all thrown overboard. In the water, at first, I could hold my breath and come up for air, then suddenly I was pulled into a rip current that sucked me down. Then I would be set free, come up for air, swim, and the whole thing would happen again. Until I got caught in a whirlpool that didn't release me."

"That's when I felt it happen," said Husseina.

"Twins! You are powerful."

"It's not us. It's Yemanjá. She saved us."

"Why do you think that?" asked Hassana. "How do you know that?"

"I was so far away from you, so there's no way I could see. Maybe the moment you started drowning was when I went into a trance. Yemanjá took over and led me into the water. I told her we didn't want to join her. Not yet."

"Did you see Yemanjá?" Hassana asked.

Husseina shook her head.

"Then how do you know it's real? Anyone could imagine what I was going through."

"I still can't swim, Hassana. If I had control of what I was doing, I wouldn't have gone into the water. I don't need to see her to believe in her. At first, I thought *I* was the one drowning, then the memories came—of your mission home, of Accra. I realized they weren't mine."

"And why would she send you into the water and not just save me?"

"Yemanjá likes to keep her children close. I fought for us to stay alive."

Hassana looked at her plate, drew circles with her fork.

"I *am* a strong swimmer," she said. "I can control water. And yet this is the second time in my life I've almost drowned. The other time, I was trying to save a girl who couldn't swim and she sucked me down with her. It wasn't even deep water. This time it was deep. In books I've read, people describing near-death always mention a tunnel. I saw a pinprick of light. Suddenly, I was on the shore and you were there by me."

"There are things in life you can't control," Husseina said.

Hassana said nothing.

"I've had this dream my whole life. I didn't know it was about you. I'd always thought *I* would drown."

"And the others?" Tereza asked, sitting back in her chair.

"From where I stood, it looked as if, apart from the people who made it back to the steamer, Hassana and the Kru men were the only ones that the sea didn't take." Husseina turned from Tereza to Hassana. "Yemanjá protects us and seamen: fishermen, sailors, dockers... There are sharks in that water. It's a miracle that you—we—survived."

"Where you might have a point," said Hassana, "is how, before I started fading, there was a moment when I stopped struggling—it was as if I were breathing in water. I became fishlike."

"Yemanjá!" both Tereza and Husseina exclaimed.

Tereza shot up and clapped.

Hassana watched them both and shifted her gaze to her plate again.

"I think *you* saved me. Your belief in Yemanjá just made you strong enough to go in the water," she said. "Listen, we don't have to believe in the same things. I am just happy to be here and alive and with you."

Husseina watched the muscles in her sister's cheeks quiver. It was true that she had to be patient with Hassana, even if her sister never became a believer. Then it hit her: Hassana *did* believe in something.

"Thank *you* for believing in our dreams."

"And thank you," said Hassana, "for saving me."

They looked at each other and smiled. Hassana's smile wide and toothy. Husseina's close-lipped and warm.

ACKNOWLEDGEMENTS

I owe a big thank you to Sarah Odedina and the incredible team at Pushkin Children's Books for pulling this gem of a story out of me and for sending it out into the world. Thank you, Maria and Anna of Pontas Agency, for continuing to champion my work. Thank you, Jori and Ciku, for your humour, your feedback, and delicious home-cooked meals. Thank you, Fawzia, for bending me into shape and for listening to me talk *sans cesse* about the girls. Thank you, the Gee, especially Irene and Kuorkor, for the one line I bugged you about and, of course, for friendship. Thank you, Pierre, Emile, Nana, Monsieur, Rahma and Annie for the gift of family and encouragement. And finally, thank you, dear reader, for following the girls on their quest to find each other.

TEEN AND YA FICTION

*Available and coming soon
from Pushkin Press*

BEARMOUTH
Liz Hyder

**THE DISAPPEARANCES
SPLINTERS OF SCARLET**
Emily Bain Murphy

**THE BEAST PLAYER
THE BEAST WARRIOR**
Nahoko Uehashi

GLASS TOWN WARS
Celia Rees

THE MURDERER'S APE
Jakob Wegelius

THE BEGINNING WOODS
Malcolm McNeill

THE COLLECTIVE
Lindsey Whitlock